jean m'baraï

THE trepang fisherman

GEORGES BAUDOUX'S

Jean m'baraï

THE trepang fisherman

TRANSLATED AND WITH A
CRITICAL INTRODUCTION

BY KARIN SPEEDY

PUBLICATION INFORMATION

UTS ePRESS
University of Technology Sydney
Sydney NSW 2007
AUSTRALIA
epress.lib.uts.edu.au

Copyright Information

This book is copyright. The work is licensed under a
Creative Commons Attribution-Non Commercial-Non Derivatives License
CC BY-NC-ND

http://creativecommons.org/licenses/by-nc-nd/4.0/

First Published 2015
© 2015 in the text, Karin Speedy
© 2015 in the cover artwork, book artwork, design and layout, Emily Gregory and UTS ePRESS

Publication Details

DOI citation: http://dx.doi.org/10.5130/978-0-9945039-1-6

Creator: Baudoux, Georges, 1870-1949, author.
Other Creators/Contributors: Speedy, Karin, translator, writer of introduction.
Title: Georges Baudoux's Jean M'Baraï the trepang fisherman /
Translated and with a critical introduction by Karin Speedy.

ISBN: 9780994503916 (ebook)
ISBN: 9780994503923 (paperback)

Subjects: New Caledonian fiction (French) – Translations into English.
New Caledonian fiction (French) – Translations into English—History and criticism.

Dewey Number: 843.8

UTS ePRESS

Manager: Julie-Anne Marshall
Book Editor: Matthew Noble
Design: Emily Gregory
Enquiries: utsepress@uts.edu.au

For enquiries about third party copyright material reproduced in this work, please contact UTS ePRESS.

OPEN ACCESS

UTS ePRESS publishes peer reviewed books, journals and conference proceedings and is the leading publisher of peer reviewed open access journals in Australasia. All UTS ePRESS online content is free to access and read.

CULTURALLY SENSITIVE INFORMATION

*Aboriginal and Torres Strait Islander people, and people of the
Melanesian, Micronesian and Polynesian islands, should be aware
that this book contains images of people who are now deceased.*

TABLE OF CONTENTS

LIST OF MAPS AND IMAGES

MAPS

IMAGES

CRITICAL INTRODUCTION :
colonial voices from the french pacific

BY KARIN SPEEDY

I have only one language; it is not mine.

Jacques Derrida[1]

The relentless imperatives of colonialism and empire have split the traditionally linguistically diverse, yet closely connected Pacific region, into two main literary producing spheres: one francophone, the other anglophone. Until recently, these two islands of discourse, while geographically close, have not been able to engage in meaningful exchange due to linguistic distance.

While often addressing similar themes, with both parallels and specificities on historical, cultural, linguistic and literary levels, francophone Pacific literature has remained on the outer, if not consciously so, in what has come to be known as the genre or discipline of Pacific literature. This literature, comprising for the most part indigenous or local literary production published from the 1960s, has been taught in anglophone universities in the Pacific region since the late 1970s. Seen as regional, if not marginal, by institutions housed within yet on the periphery of English departments, it has almost exclusively been a literature in English.

For many readers or students of Pacific literature, then, francophone perspectives on

---

1   Derrida (1998).

the shared and contrasting Pacific experiences of colonisation, conflict and the search for identity have often passed unnoticed. The late New Zealand poet and academic Ken Arvidson identified this francophone absence from the genre in his article on the history of Pacific literature. He writes:

> *I am conscious in writing this, by the way, of what a large area of the south-west Pacific is occluded by considering only the anglophone sector. What interaction is there between the anglophone and francophone sectors? It is hard to believe societies as dynamic as those of Tahiti and New Caledonia do not impact on the rest of the region. But for all the traces there are of them in anglophone South Pacific literature, they might as well be on another planet. [. . .] francophone literature, even if there is some in English translation, is a complete black hole in our understanding of what south Pacific writing is (Arvidson 1999/2009, 104-105).*

The lack of any kind of developed dialogue between the two literary spheres is rooted in (post)colonial linguistic difference. The Derridean concept of the monolingualism of the Other, the paradox whereby colonised peoples find their own voices through the medium of the coloniser's language, has seen the flourishing of new monolingual literatures in the Pacific. While these literatures bear witness to the historical *métissage* of their genesis, their writers weaving the patterns, rhythms, tones, vocabulary and structures of their ancestral tongues into those of the colonisers, their monolingual nature has created a barrier to mutual intelligibility across the Pacific.

When we consider the historical connections between Pacific peoples, the migrations[2] (both pre- and post-European contact), and reflect on the role of language in these encounters, we understand that this linguistic barrier is but an artifice of colonialism. Despite, or perhaps because of, linguistic diversity, intra-Pacific dialogues were once possible. Indeed, even when Europeans entered the region, Polynesian languages[3] served for many years as vehicles of communication and exchange throughout Oceania. The similarities between Reo Mā'ohi and Te Reo Māori, for instance, meant that Tahitian chief, priest and navigator, Tupaia, was able to interpret for Captain James Cook in his dealings with New Zealand Māori.[4]

---

2   Epeli Hau'ofa famously described the Pacific, or Oceania, as a "sea of islands", reflecting the way in which Pacific peoples had viewed their environment over the past 2000 years. Their great skill in navigating led to migration, trade and cultural exchange. He writes:

> *Theirs was a large world in which peoples and cultures moved and mingled unhindered by boundaries of the kind erected much later by imperial powers. From one island to another they sailed to trade and to marry, thereby expanding social networks for greater flow of wealth. They travelled to visit relatives in a wide variety of natural and cultural surroundings, to quench their thirst for adventure, and even to fight and dominate (Hau'ofa_1994, 153-154).*

3   Polynesian languages belong to the same language family and while they naturally developed in different directions over time and space, they share sufficient similarities to allow communication between different groups of speakers. They thus served as lingua francas in the Pacific. In New Caledonia, for instance, prior to European contact, groups of Polynesians arrived at different times and settled in Uvea (where Fagauvea, a Polynesian language, is still spoken today) and along the East Coast of New Caledonia. Polynesian languages were therefore spoken in New Caledonia and some lexical items entered the local Melanesian languages. When the first Europeans arrived in New Caledonia, communication was facilitated by the presence of these Polynesian languages and speakers who sometimes acted as interpreters. In Balade, in the north-east of New Caledonia, a type of pidgin Polynesian (Maritime Polynesian Pidgin as described by Drechsel 2007) was used as the language of communication between Kanak, European explorers, missionaries and traders (Hollyman 1959, 2000a).

4   See Te Punga Somerville (2012) for Tupaia's story and a fascinating study on Māori-Pasifika identity through their connections to the ocean.

And, in the push to evangelise the Pacific, the London Missionary Society employed native teachers (Tahitians, Samoans, Rarotongans) to conquer the souls of diverse Polynesian and Melanesian peoples. The teachers, themselves great linguists, brought "the Word" to their converts, initially via the medium of a Polynesian contact language. As a result of earlier migrations, vestiges of Polynesian languages remained in Melanesian islands such as New Caledonia. These traces of previous contact were sufficient to enable, if not fully-fledged conversations, then at least the beginnings of a dialogue between the missionary teachers and their target pupils. Polynesian pidgins were in turn picked up by European traders, adventurers, whalers, beachcombers and sandalwooders, whose interactions with indigenous peoples led to the development of beach-la-mar (or bichelamar), a contact language based on varieties of Polynesian, Melanesian and English, a language which functioned as a colonial conduit between European and Oceanic worlds throughout much of the 19th century.[5]

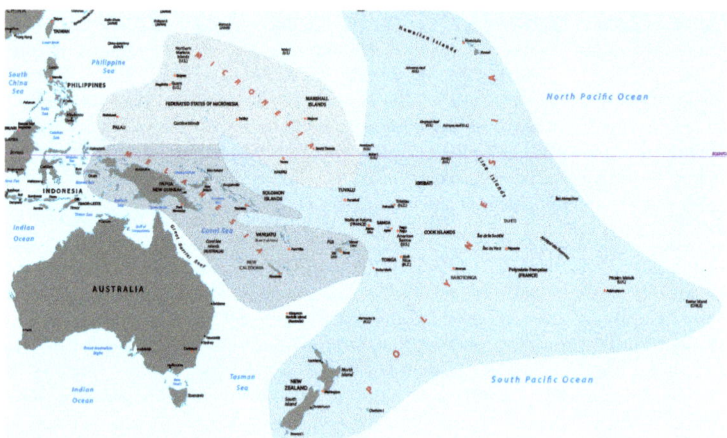

MAP 1: THE PACIFIC OCEAN AND ITS PEOPLES

In the 21st century, the so-called globalised era, it is more than a little ironic then, that in the Pacific region, the descendants of Tupaia and the New Caledonian converts are speaking and writing in French, while those of the Māori and the native teachers are speaking and writing in English. The former Pacific interconnectedness has been unravelled by indigenous language loss, or in other words, the violent imposition of the monolingualism of the Other. Now, despite movements of indigenous language revitalisation and the publication of some literary texts in various Pacific languages,[6] the postcolonial impasse

---

5   See Hollyman (1959) for a discussion on Polynesian migration and linguistic influence in New Caledonia and the development of beach-la-mar.

6   While indigenous language texts play an important role in linguistic and cultural renewal, the tradition of societal multilingualism that was once prevalent in the Pacific, particularly in Melanesia, is giving way to the monolingualism of the Other and, consequently, these indigenous language texts do not have an impact outside of their local and diasporic communities.

remains; francophone and anglophone Pacific literatures cannot speak to each other... Or can they?

RECOVERING VOICES OF THE PAST

Over the past decade there has been a turn, in academic circles at least, towards a broader Pacific literary vision. The same linguistic constraints remain: Pacific literature continues to be hosted within monolingual literature departments and is taught to essentially monolingual students, a situation that has proved a stumbling block for a field that has perhaps always had bi-/multi-lingual aspirations. What has changed, however, is the increasing availability via translation of a small number of francophone Pacific literary texts. Academics teaching Pacific literature in the region have been able to incorporate some of these francophone voices into their courses. Some anglophone students have thus had the opportunity to read writers such as Chantal Spitz, Déwé Gorodé or the various Tahitian authors in the translated anthology Varua Tupu.[7] And anglophone scholars have expressed willingness to include more translated francophone texts in their teaching, provided they are readily available at a reasonable cost.[8]

It is perhaps pertinent to mention here, by way of comparison, the situation in the francophone Pacific universities. Both the University of New Caledonia (Noumea) and the University of French Polynesia (Punaauia, Tahiti) offer courses in anglophone Pacific literature. These courses are housed within English departments, which are, of course, Foreign Language departments in these institutions. Their appellation, "Anglophone Pacific Literature", identifies them as foreign, Other. It would thus seem that the notion of a singular / universal Pacific literature encompassing both anglophone and francophone spheres has not yet found a space within these universities either. Of course, the tyranny of the monolingualism of the Other means that, just as anglophone literature students cannot be expected to read French texts, francophone literature students cannot be asked to read English.[9]

Moving beyond the realms of academia to the readers and writers themselves (although the fact that many Pacific literary figures are scholars / writers blurs things around the edges somewhat), it is also useful to consider who is reading whom in the Pacific. Pointing out the limited scope writers have for literary exchange due to the "linguistic divide", Jean Anderson makes the following observation:

> *English being the current 'lingua franca' of the globe, French Pacific writers are more*
> *likely to have some awareness of their English-language counterparts than vice-versa,*
> *although it is clear that reading literature, rather than toaster instructions or emails,*

---

7   It must be noted that this contact with Francophone literature, while encouraging, has so far been minimal. Alice Te Punga Somerville (Victoria University, Wellington and now University of Hawai'i) continues to teach Jean Anderson's translation of Chantal Spitz's Island of Shattered Dreams. When I spoke with Robert Sullivan (University of Hawai'i) and Selena Tusitala Marsh (University of Auckland) in 2010, neither was using Francophone texts in their teaching but mentioned previous engagement with Varua Tupu and Déwé Gorodé in their classes. For more details see Speedy 2015b.

8   These academics mentioned that they had had to drop the glossy anthology Varua Tupu from their course reading lists due to its considerable expense for students.

9   Neither of these universities offers Anglophone Pacific texts in translation as part of a more general literary degree.

requires the kind of high-level foreign language skills few of us actually acquire, in order to fully appreciate finer nuances (Anderson 2010, 288)

The crux of the matter lies therein. In order for the two literary communities to have the kinds of mutually nourishing conversations that would undoubtedly enrich the genre, they need to be able to read each other. Realistically, this can only happen through translation.

The act of translating Pacific literatures, however, is not without problems. Ideologically, it appears somewhat incongruous to think that the only way these literatures can converse is through the filter of not one but two colonial tongues (French and English). On the other hand, of course, neither literature as we know it could exist if divorced from its monolingual (yet hybrid) condition. In fact, the concept of a single regional French / English monolingualism is illusory. The reality is far more complex. Each francophone and anglophone country / territory has its own form of monolingualism, the result of the particular social, historical, and linguistic conditions under which it evolved. Various substrates, superstrates and adstrates[10] were woven together in these individual loci of contact, leading to the creation of not only specific idioms (New Caledonian French, Tahitian French, Fijian English, Samoan English, Hawaiian English, New Zealand English etc.) but also unique literatures. Under the umbrella of the universal, then, shelters a great many singularities.[11] And it is precisely these singularities, these signifiers of identity, which also make the task of a translator of Pacific literature especially demanding.

Taking up the challenge is a group of francophone scholars working out of New Zealand and Australian universities who, as passionate readers of, and engaged researchers in, both literary traditions, aim to help bridge the linguistic distance between the literary islands. Jean Anderson of Victoria University of Wellington (New Zealand) has translated Tahitian writers Chantal Spitz and Moetai Brotherson and New Caledonian poets Nicolas Kurtovitch, Paul Wamo and Frédéric Ohlen.[12] I have translated New Caledonian settler writers Hélène Savoie[13] and Georges Baudoux. Raylene Ramsay and Deborah Walker from the University of Auckland (New Zealand) have translated New Caledonian writer Déwé Gorodé, as has Peter Brown from the Australian National University. Ramsay and Walker have also jointly edited / translated Nights of Storytelling. A Cultural History of Kanaky / New Caledonia, an important volume that provides an overview of New Caledonian writing through the translation of a variety of historical and contemporary texts.[14] Much, much more work remains to be done but we should see this as a positive start in a movement towards a broader, more representative conceptualisation of Pacific literature.

With the exception of some of the historical texts in Ramsay and Walker's collection and my translation of an excerpt from Georges Baudoux's short story "Sauvages et civilisés" (Speedy 2003), the majority of the above-mentioned translated texts were written in the late 20th

---

10   In the context of contact languages, superstrates are the languages of power (languages of the colonisers), substrates are the languages of the colonised peoples and the term adstrate is used when there is contact between languages of social equality (see Smith 2015, 262).

11   Jean Baudrillard's famous concept of the superposition of the singular, universal and global, with the singular always inhabiting the universal, springs to mind (Baudrillard 2003).

12   Teaming up with France Grenaudier-Klijn (Massey University, New Zealand), Anderson has also translated New Zealand Māori writer Patricia Grace into French.

13   Marie Ramsland also translated a volume of Savoie's poetry in 1998.

14   For references to all of these works, see the bibliography.

or early 21st centuries.[15] While they can certainly be appreciated on their own merits, the dearth of earlier francophone Pacific literature in translation means that anglophone readers lack a context against which they can read them as part of an ongoing dialogue within their own literary tradition. They are unable to make the kinds of connections, identify acts of "writing back" (cf. Ashcroft, Griffiths and Tiffin 1989) that they can when reading, say, Robert Louis Stevenson or Albert Wendt. For anglophone readers to begin to appreciate the interplay between past and present, to have any hope of recognising intertextuality, literary rule-breaking, hybridisation etc., it is essential that some of the translation effort be directed to the works of early colonial / postcolonial writers. For, without access to the early texts, it is difficult to read the works of contemporary writers within their specific postcolonial context.

The objective of this book, then, is to introduce New Caledonia's first writer, Georges Baudoux, to the English-speaking readers of Pacific literature via the translation of "Jean M'Baraï le pêcheur de tripangs", his longest story and one of his most interesting ones from the viewpoint of francophone-anglophone Pacific connections.

GEORGES BAUDOUX, 1920

---

15 Jean Mariotti's Contes de Poindi (1939), which contains only one tale, was published in French and English in parallel by the same American publisher. The English version, Tales of Poindi (1938), was translated by Esther Holden Averill (O'Reilly 1949, 191).

GEORGES BAUDOUX – SETTLER EXTRAORDINAIRE

Georges Baudoux, the francophone Pacific's answer to Stevenson and Melville according to his first biographer Patrick O'Reilly (O'Reilly 1950, 204), differed from his anglophone counterparts in that, unlike them, he lived almost his entire life in the Pacific. He had a profound attachment to both his adopted land and the individuals who inhabited it. These people, amalgams of real men and women he had met and meticulously observed throughout his life of adventure in the New Caledonian bush – Kanak, métis (half-castes), settlers, indentured workers, stockmen, convicts, broussards (bushmen), miners, sailors, fishermen, etc. – would populate his stories and lend to them the ring of "authenticity" for which they have long been lauded.[16]

Although Baudoux portrayed himself more as a reporter on New Caledonian colonial life, a transcriber or translator of tales, he was a real story-teller with an impressive flair for recounting the narratives of the island, giving voices of sorts to all its residents. Without denying the inextricable colonial elements, flavours and ideologies present in his work, he was the first writer to focus on the local and write from an insider's viewpoint. This was an important step in the creation of a New Caledonian literature, a literature that would generate its own foundation myths, paving the way towards the eventual emergence of a postcolonial New Caledonian literature.[17]

Georges Baudoux was, in many ways, the typical pioneering settler. In his personal exploits and in his literature, he promulgated the myth of the settler-pioneer: the strong, audacious, courageous, civilised man who, through hard physical labour, would tame the savage, chaotic land and people to create a new, ordered colonial space. For Eddy Banaré, "the most profound singularity of Baudoux's work is in his experience of colonisation" (Banaré 2010, 245).[18] And this is why, as Alain Solier points out, it is impossible to truly appreciate his writing without knowing about his life, a life in which he "proved, in his younger days, he was 'capable of…'" troca fishing, discovering mines or working as a stockman (1996, 5).

Born in 1870 in the 18th arrondissement in Paris, Georges Baudoux (pronounced Baudoucks) arrived in New Caledonia in 1875.[19] His father, François, who had previously worked as a printer, was in the army and, following the 1871 uprising of the Paris Commune, was assigned to guard the Communards who were destined for the penal colony (le bagne) of New Caledonia. Georges and his mother Marguerite accompanied François and the Communard prisoners aboard the old frigate the Virginie. On the way to New Caledonia, the ship stopped in Brazil where Georges' parents bought him a little hand-made iron saucepan – a memento that he held onto until his death in 1949.

The family lived attached to the penal colony installations on the île des Pins and the île Nou before moving to Noumea in 1882.

---

16 See the following section, however, for a critique of this claimed "authenticity".

17 See Speedy (2006) for a discussion on these themes in relation to the short story "Sauvages et civilisés".

18 Eddy Banaré's thesis was published in 2012 (Banaré 2012). All translations of the French critical literature are my own.

19 The biographical information on Georges Baudoux in this section comes principally from O'Reilly (1950) and Gasser (1996) unless otherwise referenced.

POINT ARTILLERY,
NOUMEA, NEW
CALEDONIA, 1905

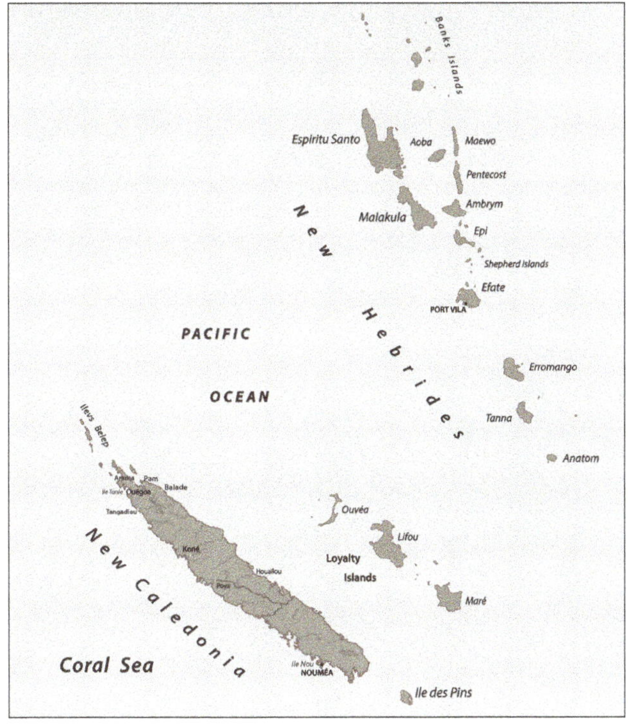

MAP 2: NEW CALEDONIA AND NEW HEBRIDES (VANUATU) PEOPLES

Baudoux led an apparently idyllic childhood, having the freedom to go off on walks, fishing or gathering fruit, discovering the New Caledonian flora and fauna of the coast and the bush. He went to the prison school and was taught by a series of Communard detainees. His classmates were mostly children of the prisoners. He learned the "three Rs" before leaving at twelve years of age to work in the printing trade. Baudoux joined the newspaper Le Moniteur de la Nouvelle-Calédonie, going from selling papers on the streets to writing copy within a year. It was from this time that he began his lifelong passion for reading. And, it was also when he was introduced to what would eventually become the subject of his fiction – the daily events and oddities of the colony, the news items in which the settlers, convicts and Kanak were the major actors (cf. Banaré 2010, 243).

Baudoux's taste for adventure and communing with nature developed further during his teenage years. He learned to sail and bought himself a little boat, the Surprise, which he used for fishing and exploring the coasts. He hunted and hiked around the island, getting to know the landscape intimately. In 1888, following the death of his father, Georges, his mother and his sister moved up to the north of the colony, settling in Koné. Like his future (semi)-fictional character Jean M'Baraï, Baudoux earned his living fishing for trepang (bêche-de-mer or sea cucumber), a sought-after commodity in East Asia. These were the days when he came into contact with many of the New Caledonians who would provide the raw material for his stories; freed convicts, pioneers, and Kanak. There were also romantic adventures with pretty "popinées" (the term used in colonial times to designate Kanak women) and beautiful, sensuous métisses, encounters he would later relate in stories such as "Pastorale calédonienne" (A New Caledonian Pastoral) and "Sauvages et civilisés" (The Savages and the Civilised).[20] He continued to read, teaching himself all he could about ancient mythology from the Larousse dictionary, the only book he had on board his boat.

WAYSIDE SCENE,
NEW CALEDONIA,
CA 1906

---

20 Most of Baudoux's stories have not been translated so I have provided fairly literal translations of their titles in parentheses for the benefit of the reader. These titles may not reflect those chosen by future translators in future translations.

Tiring of fishing, attracted by the rough and ready life of the stockmen he had met in the north, Baudoux became, for a time, one of them. His experience taming wild horses, driving herds of cattle and chasing runaway stock through the bush, again provided him with a wealth of memories that he would later bring to life in his stories. The Kanak legends that the indigenous workers told around the campfire at night were filed away for future reference. O'Reilly tells us that Baudoux "listened to them, interested. He questioned them. And, little by little, he began to familiarise himself with the secrets of their ways" (O'Reilly 1950, 190).[21]

While this active, outdoors lifestyle appealed to Baudoux, he was always on the lookout for new experiences and opportunities. Mining was to give him not only another pool of personalities and escapades from where he could draw his stories, but also make him his fortune.[22] Employing both freed and runaway convicts, ex-sailors and drifters as well as Kanak from the New Hebrides (Vanuatu), Baudoux was able, through a combination of force and humanity, to manage his sometimes volatile staff and turn his mines (Bellacossia, Damoclès, Tamatave, Fridoline and Asie) and his store to profit.

A MINE IN PILOU, NEAR ARAMA AND PAM, NORTHERN NEW CALEDONIA, CA 1900

---

21   This and all subsequent translations are my own.

22   See Banaré (2010, 2012) for a discussion on Baudoux's contribution to the body of New Caledonian literature that focuses on mining.

Baudoux also began to write poetry at this time and later, in 1913, he penned his first short-story, "Comment on s'évadait de la Nouvelle-Calédonie" (How We Escaped from New Caledonia). He wrote this yarn in convict slang. His first published writing, however, consisted of the job advertisements for miners that he placed in the newspapers.[23] Written in a picturesque type of French designed to echo the speech of the local mining community, these advertisements demonstrated the talent for transcribing spoken idioms he would later show in his stories. The advertisements proved very successful.

Life in the bush, however, was precarious and Baudoux was to learn of the danger of this isolation in the most painful of ways. With the nearest doctor some 100 kilometres away, his children were struck down with diphtheria. Franck, the baby died and, after burying his son, Baudoux rode through the night, carrying his daughter Aline, to Koné where she received treatment and survived. His marriage to his first wife Jeanne, however, did not. The couple divorced in 1902, due partly to the loss of Franck and partly to Baudoux's affairs.

Georges married again two years later, made a trip to France then returned to the bush and the mines. He mined the Kataviti mine in Koné until 1914 when the chrome crisis struck and he sold up and set sail for France again. This trip was aborted in Sydney – the First World War had broken out and he was stuck in Australia for eighteen months.

(L) JEANNE BAUDOUX, GEORGES'S FIRST WIFE, 1900

(R) MARIE BAUDOUX, GEORGES'S SECOND WIFE, CA 1910

---

23   "Acré aux Cobaleurs", one of these job advertisements was reproduced in O'Reilly (1950, 191).

GEORGES (LEFT) BUILDING HIS HOUSE IN HOUAILOU, NEW CALEDONIA, CA 1920

Upon his return to New Caledonia, Baudoux and his wife Marie bought a house in Noumea where, in his mid-forties, the action man of the bush turned to writing. Periods of intense production alternated with lulls in his output; the vast majority of his stories were written between the two World Wars. Widowed in 1927, he decided to follow his son Georges to the bush in 1928, buying a property in Houaïlou and building a house. He would live there almost until the end of his life. He continued to write and collect legends from the Kanak living around Houaïlou. During the Second World War, Baudoux stopped writing. His son had joined the Free French Forces and Baudoux stepped in to help look after his grandchildren. In 1948, when his son moved with his family to Port Vila (Vanuatu), Baudoux returned to Noumea, renting a room in the Lapérouse Hotel. It was there that he saw his ex-wife Jeanne again for the last time – the two had maintained contact over the years. Despite the divorce, Baudoux, it was said, never stopped loving her. It was also there that on 5 July 1949, Georges Baudoux, New Caledonia's first writer, died, ill and alone, of a heart attack.

WRITING THE VOICES OF COLONISATION

I write stories. I know so many! I manage to detach myself, to think of nothing other than my subject. I see my past before me, the things I felt and experienced, the bitterness has gone. It's a healthy pastime. I throw myself into it for hours on end. Thoughts come… They are youthful reminiscences… dreams.

- Georges Baudoux[24]

While Georges Baudoux had doubtlessly pursued every opportunity the settler lifestyle had to offer, drinking in the essence of the colony and its peoples, writing was initially for him a personal and mostly private activity. He did not plan to publish his stories. In fact, he was apparently bullied into surrendering his manuscripts to Auguste and Alin Laubreaux, the father and son who founded the literary newspaper Le Messager de la Nouvelle-Calédonie in 1918.[25] Instead of returning the stories to Baudoux after they had read them (as they had promised), the Laubreaux proceeded to publish them. The first instalment of "Kaavo",[26] one of Baudoux's Kanak legends, appeared as the first in a series entitled "Légendes noires des chaînes" (Black Legends from the Mountain Chains) in Le Messager, no. 9 on 26 February 1919. The stories were signed "Thiosse", a transcription of the Kanak pronunciation of Georges. Other stories, "Ce vieux Tchiao" (That Old Tchiao), "Flirt canaque" (Kanak Flirtation) and "Pastorale calédonienne" (A New Caledonian Pastoral) followed one after the next and his longest stories, "Jean M'Baraï, le pêcheur de tripangs" (Jean M'Baraï the Trepang Fisherman) and 'Le Taureau de Bargen" (The Bull of Bargen), were also published in 1919 and 1920 respectively by Le Messager.

Highlighting, in the most glowing terms, the literary and documentary qualities of "Thiosse's" stories, Alin Laubreaux prefaced "Légendes noires des chaînes" (Black Legends from the Mountain Chains) with the following words:

You have been able, before and better than anyone else could have, to find the savage poetry that was sleeping at the bottom of New Caledonia's mountain ranges and gorges. You have described confidently, realistically and sometimes extensively, the strange, original spirit of the indigenous populations – the Kanak, popinées, half-castes and poor wretches. [. . .]Your words rouse the exclamation, "Yes, it's just like that!" [. . .] Your scenes of the daily life of New Caledonian stockmen, quite apart from their literary qualities, have documentary value due to their precision and realism. Your "Kaavo" is a masterpiece and at times when reading it I felt the grandiose presence of a genius who is unaware of his talent.[27]

While Baudoux was not the first writer to feature in serialised form in the New Caledonian newspapers, he was the first to write about life in the colony, the first to have New Caledonia and its diverse populations as his primary subject matter (Banaré 2010, 252). The readers of Le Messager were enchanted and Baudoux quickly became famous in both Noumea and

---

24 A letter from Baudoux to his daughter Aline, who lived in Paris, dated 1920 (O'Reilly 1950, 194).
25 Unless referenced otherwise, most of the biographical detail of this section is drawn from O'Reilly (1950) and Gasser (1996).
26 Kaavo is the name of the daughter of the chief of the Témala clan.
27 In O'Reilly (1950, 194-195).

the bush.

Le Messager ceased to exist from 1921 when Alin Laubreaux left for France. But Baudoux's serialised stories were taken up by Le Bulletin du Commerce de la Nouvelle-Calédonie. From September 1923 to May 1924, Le Bulletin du Commerce published "La vocation d'Angèle" (Angèle's Vocation), "Le Tayo gras" (The Fat Tayo),[28] "Le Médium" (The Medium), "Nocturne calédonien en 1894" (New Caledonian Nocture in 1894), which later became "L'Emprise du crime" (Born Criminal) and "Comment on s'évadait de la Nouvelle-Calédonie" (How We Escaped from New Caledonia). The following year, "Autrefois chez les broussards" (The Old Days among the Bushmen) appeared in the left-wing newspaper Le Démocrate de la Nouvelle-Calédonie et dependences and Auguste Laubreaux made Baudoux the first New Caledonian fiction writer to be published in book form with the collection Légendes noires. Mœurs canaques (Black Legends. Kanak Traditions) that was published in Noumea in 1925.

(L) COVER OF HOW WE ESCAPED FROM NEW CALEDONIA (2001 EDITION)

(R) COVER OF KANAK LEGENDS VOLUME 1 (1952 EDITION)

Over the next few years Baudoux would write only two more stories, "Le Dugong" (The Dugong) and "Les tribulations de M. Boisdésil" (The Trials and Tribulations of Monsieur Boisdésil).[29] "Le Dugong" was included in the collection Légendes canaques

---

28 The word "tayo" came into use in New Caledonia via Polynesian and subsequently via its use in the local pidgin and it means "friend". In colonial New Caledonia "tayo" designated the Kanak man as opposed to "popinée" (from the Polynesian "wahine") that was used to designate the Kanak woman (see Speedy 2013b, 200).

29 Boisdésil is an example of word play. The name sounds like bois des îles or wood from the islands. This story has never been published.

(Kanak Legends), published in Paris in 1928 with a preface by the famous anthropologist Lucien Lévy-Bruhl. Sales in Paris were, however, disappointing. Doubtlessly stung by the plagiarism of his former publisher Alin Laubreaux whose Yann-le-métis, published in Paris in 1928 was an inferior and thinly veiled rip-off of "Jean M'Baraï", and drained by the ensuing court case, which lasted six years, Baudoux withdrew from the literary scene. In 1935, the court case won, Baudoux took up writing again with "La Poisse" (Bad Luck), a timely story featuring a Jewish settler in the North who was jinxed, "Justice Express" and "Clotho". These stories were not published until 1979. In 1938, his friend Edmond Cané persuaded him to contribute some stories to the new journal Études mélanésiennes and in 1938 the Kanak legend "L'Invasion sournoise" (The Insidious Invasion) appeared followed by the last story to be published in his lifetime, "L'Épouvante" (The Horror), in 1939. Baudoux wrote two more Kanak legends 'Kavino" (1939) and "Le Trou symbolique" (The Symbolic Hole) (1940), both of which appeared in 1952 in Légendes canaques 1 and 2 respectively. His final stories, "Première récompense scolaire" (First School Award) and "Le Pont d'Avignon" (The Avignon Bridge), which Baudoux did not finish, were written in 1940 and were also published posthumously in 1979.

From the mid-1920s, Baudoux, who had embraced the fame that had accidentally come his way, felt somewhat neglected by his readers and was rather bemused to have received much of his more recent critical acclaim from the missionaries in the colony. In 1926 he wrote:

> *Here the missionaries, priests and pastors see my stories as important. They talk to me about them often [. . .] their appreciation is touching. They know the Kanak soul. They tell me that it comes through well in the psychological details in my stories, they say that my descriptions are like real life, like photographs.*[30]

One of these missionaries was the pastor Maurice Leenhardt. Leenhardt and Baudoux had most likely met in Noumea in 1919 during the trials for the participants of the 1917 Kanak Revolt.[31] The pastor (who was also an ethnologist and linguist) and the writer developed a relationship of mutual respect and appreciation, based, according to Baudoux's second biographer Bernard Gasser, on the fact that "both men were among the rare Europeans in 1919 who understood Kanak and who liked them enormously" (Gasser 1996, 29). Leenhardt would later include a lengthy description of a "pilou" (ceremonial Kanak dance) taken from Baudoux's "Kaavo" in his 1937 ethnological study Gens de la Grande-Terre.[32]

Leenhardt also passed Baudoux's stories on to his Parisian colleague Lucien Lévy-Bruhl. Lévy-Bruhl not only praised the New Caledonian author for his "truthful" and "objective" writing and vaunted the "authentic" quality of his descriptions of Kanak life in his preface for *Légendes canaques*, but he also made use of these descriptions of the Kanak Other in his own work (*La mentalité primitive* published in 1922). In an excerpt from his preface, the

---

30 In O'Reilly (1950 ,198).
31 This revolt rocked the colonial society that believed it had "pacified" the indigenous population following the repression of the 1878 Revolt and subsequent institution of the harsh Indigenous Code in 1887. The reports of the supposedly extinct "primitive" practice of cannibalism during the 1917 Revolt horrified Noumean society. Baudoux, writing for Le Messager, condemned the acts of cannibalism labeling them "inhuman" (Gasser 1996, 29). See Bensa, Goromoedo and Muckle (2015) for a recent interdisciplinary study of the 1917 revolt.
32 See Leenhardt (1986, 159).

impact Baudoux's "scientific" descriptions had on the anthropologist is evident. He writes:

> *The image that he gives us of the New Caledonian Kanak is not spoiled by any retouching made for literary purposes. He sketches them before us, lifelike snapshots, as he saw them, without making them either more or less complicated than what they are. For many long years he lived near them, with them – which is essential to gain their confidence and not misinterpret them. [...] In this way, he has been able to penetrate quite deeply into the soul of these Melanesians. His "popinées" and their men live as they do in real life. [...] His scrupulous accuracy, far from being detrimental to his work, makes it all the more poignant. His sincerity will earn him praise from the general public without displeasing those who know.*[33]

With acclaim from the scientific community and the award of the Palmes Académiques,[34] Baudoux's legend, that of the voice of some kind of New Caledonian truth or essence, the creator of a New Caledonian identity through his true to life writings, began to fossilize.[35]

A MELANESIAN "CASE" (HOUSE/HUT), NEW CALEDONIA, CA 1906

Yet, just as we now see in the so-called objective, scientific ethnographic studies of the time, when we examine Baudoux's stories today, we cannot help but notice the overwhelming presence of colonial ideologies and the inevitable lapse into colonial stereotype (cf. Bensa 2006). In the Kanak legends that were long upheld as accurate depictions of Kanak mores and culture, Baudoux surrenders to the sensationalism of the colonial genre. Violent scenes

---

33   In Gasser (1996, 35).

34   A French Academic prize created by Napoleon in 1808 which recognizes major contributions to French national education and culture.

35   Baudoux's stories also received attention from historians such as Bernard Brou (1980), who saw in his legend "L'invasion sournoise" evidence proving the explorer La Pérouse had landed in New Caledonia before d'Entrecasteaux.

of savagery and cannibalism, for instance, serve to justify the colonial project – the Kanak are likened to animals or "big children" and their primitivism, brutality, superstitions and instinctive nature places them at the bottom of the scale of humanity.

In an article discussing the themes of cannibalism in Baudoux's writing, I assert:

> *[. . .] despite moments of ambivalence and a degree of empathy with the other, Baudoux's Légendes canaques are steeped in racist discourses, including the survival of the fittest and a developmental view of history, which are spelled out in his 'Author's note'. Describing himself as a transcriber of Melanesian tales (and here it could be argued that he has, in effect, cannibalised Kanak oral histories), Baudoux claims he wants to describe 'the customs of a human clan that had been held back, lingering in its primitive state, at that evolutionary stage when instincts are emerging from animality'. At the same time, displaying his apparent adherence to a monogenetic view of humanity, he points out to the 'civilised' reader that these 'unevolved cousins' are reminders of 'the reality of our origins' and by studying them, 'it is studying oneself, probing the innermost depths of one's being, and finding traces therein of these instincts that we sometimes feel welling up inside of us, without being able to explain them' (Speedy 2013a).*[36]

A NEW CALEDONIAN VILLAGE SCENE, CA 1906

---

36   Baudoux quotes taken from the 1925 Author's note reproduced in the 1952 edition of Légendes canaques.

Baudoux's hierarchical conception of society is not restricted to the black / white or savage / civilised dichotomy that is prevalent in his Kanak Legends. He extends the 19th century "scientific" theories concerning racial hierarchy and heredity to half-caste and Asian characters as well as to the white characters in his convict and mining stories. Banaré argues that this is to create a feeling of security in the young colony and to legitimise its existence. Following the example of writers such as Balzac and Zola, Baudoux "categorises criminals and convicts from all over France according to the extent to which their crime left their intelligence and humanity intact, flirting at times with the most devastating ideologies of the 20th century" (Banaré 2010, 246). Martin too notes the connection Baudoux makes between the animal, the primitive man and the criminal, suggesting that Baudoux sees in certain convicts a "regression" to a bestial state not unlike that of a savage. This notion, he advances, is based on the theories of late 19th century psychologist, Alfred Fouillée, who found psychological similarities between savages, children, hysterics and certain criminals (Martin 1995a, 372-373).

A KANAK TRIBE IN THE GORGES DU MONT MU, NEW CALEDONIA, CA 1905
(TEXT ON POSTCARD: "AS WE APPROACHED, A FEW NATIVES CAME OUT OF THEIR HUT, SEEMING TO WONDER WHAT WE WERE DOING AT THEIR PLACE")

Baudoux's paternalism, however, is symptomatic of his time and it would be unfair and anachronistic to judge him on postcolonial values. Nonetheless, it is important to deconstruct his myth as a purely documentary writer and recognise that his work is literary and hence subjective and is imbued not only with discourses of colonialism but that, in his attempt to create "a feeling of belonging" (Martin 1995a, 50) in a new land and among a new "people", he also lapses into stereotypes. This is evident in his use of language in his stories.

(L) KANAK WARRIORS, NEW CALEDONIA, CA 1906

(R) NEW CALEDONIAN WOMEN, CA 1906

(TEXT ON POSTCARD: "FOR CLOTHING, A MANOU (SKIRT) OF COCONUT FIBRES OR BANANA LEAVES, AND THAT'S ALL")

Extolled as the guardian of "la parole calédonienne" (New Caledonian speech),[37] his talent at retranscribing / reproducing / representing the linguistic particularities of his characters (their convict slang, Australian English, bichelamar, nautical jargon, "Kanak French" etc.) is what, according to O'Reilly, made his stories stand out the most, giving them "local colour and their ring of truth" (O'Reilly 1950, 198). Nevertheless, according to Martin (1995b) and Gasser (1992), this assumed linguistic authenticity, especially in relation to his reproduction of the orality of Kanak languages, is but an appearance. As a white man and "translator" of Kanak legends, Baudoux gave himself the writer's task of "the elaboration, transcription and staging of the Kanak 'word' or tradition (la parole canaque)" (Martin 1995b, 73).[38] Yet, in this supposedly objective undertaking of translation, Baudoux cannot stop himself from interrupting the transmission with his own comments and judgements. And, it is by means of literary techniques that Baudoux makes his texts more "real" (or more Kanak). Some of these techniques include the use of onomatopoeia, the doubling of words (i.e. "old, old" or "fat, fat"), interjections, accents, silences and lexemes from Kanak languages (Martin 1995b, Gasser 1992).

---

37 See Banaré (2010, 247) for details.

38 I have translated "la parole canaque" as "word" or "tradition" as its meaning extends far beyond that of the European concept of language (cf. Martin 1995b, 81-82).

Hollyman notes a number of stereotypes, especially phonological stereotypes, in Baudoux's representation of Kanak orality. While voiced prenasalised consonants are characteristic of Kanak French, Baudoux makes the error, for instance, of prenasalising an unvoiced consonant (m'pouh) (Hollyman 2000b, 90). He also fails to incorporate some of the more widespread traits of Kanak French such as the tendency to prenasalise the voiced stop consonants of French and the variation in the pronunciation of /r/ and /v/. Even where Hollyman observes several "authentic" features Baudoux has borrowed from the 19th century French pidgin that was spoken by many Kanak, he remains convinced that the French of the Kanak legends is essentially a cliché (Hollyman 2000b, 94, 98).

Similarly, my analyses of the Reunion Creole and the Vietnamese Pidgin (Tây Bôi) spoken by two characters in "Sauvages et civilisés" demonstrate that while these representations are based on reality and do contain a number of genuine elements, they are also tainted with a certain level of stereotype (Speedy 2005, 2007a, 2007b). Nonetheless, this technique, using real life as a starting point from which he could embroider his fiction, seems to work on both the literary and linguistic levels in Baudoux's stories. It certainly seems to have resonated sufficiently well with colonial New Caledonians (and even with many New Caledonians today) for them to perceive it as representative of their voice(s).

Indeed, Baudoux's use of the languages of the New Caledonian bush sets him apart from the typical colonial writer. Even though his retranscriptions are not entirely accurate – it is impossible to perfectly reproduce an oral text in written form in any case – it seems that he at least attempted to transcribe (or retranscribe) the voices of the Other, as he heard them, during his time in the bush. Unlike his colonial contemporaries who used deformed speech or animalistic sounds to represent the voices of the indigenous Other and to mark the speakers out as inferior, Baudoux, it appears, was not aiming to ridicule or poke fun in at his characters via their speech. Rather, the polyphonic nature of his stories,[39] suggests that he was trying to include all of the voices of the colonial period in his creation of an emergent New Caledonian literature.

One final point that needs to be made about Baudoux's writing is his ambiguity. As has been shown above, Baudoux's tales do not escape the colonial mindset of their writer or their period. At times, the colonial ideologies, the Social Darwinism and the discourses of conquest can be overwhelming. However, Baudoux, in stories like "L'Épouvante" (The Horror), "Jean M'Baraï" or "Sauvages et civilisés" (The Savages and the Civilised, written in 1915 but not published until 1979), also wryly and quite subversively critiques the colonial project and occasionally shows a degree of empathy for the colonised. He is able to turn his mature gaze onto his more arrogant younger self and criticise his own disregard for the destruction of the environment and the exploitation of indigenous people. He denounces the ecological devastation of mining, condemns the civilising mission with its indentured

---

39   While Baudoux allows his characters to all speak in their own languages and voice their own points of view, the polyphony is not quite in the Bakhtinian sense of the term as the author (or narrator) remains the thread that ties the characters to the story (cf. Bakhtin 1984).

labour systems[40] and the attempts to indoctrinate "pacified" colonised populations with civilised values.[41] He notes, ironically, that the only good thing civilisation has brought the indigenous people is alcohol and points out that savagery and deception is not the reserve of the primitive.[42]

A GROUP OF VILLAGERS, NEW CALEDONIA, CA 1906

In many of his stories, including some of the Kanak Legends, he also turns the ethnologist's gaze onto the whites, describing their actions and technology through Kanak eyes. The Kanak employ ethnological methods to describe the exotic white Other in relation to their own worldview. Humoristic, yet sometimes racist, this technique also underscores the ambiguity of Baudoux. While he never enters into any kind of deep analysis of colonialism and is ultimately unable to extricate himself from most colonial frameworks and stereotypes, he attempts to show a sort of universal humanity among people, or, more often than not, as we shall see in "Jean M'Baraï", a universal inhumanity that traverses all ethnic and linguistic boundaries.

---

40   After the abolition of slavery in the old colonies, colonial planters hired indentured labourers. These people (often Indians or Chinese) were contracted for a specified period of time and paid a small amount of money at the end of their indenture with the option of being repatriated or entering into another contract. While not slaves as such, many worked long hours in terrible conditions and were often subject to violence from their employers. This indenture system was adopted in the Pacific (in New Caledonia, Fiji, Samoa, Hawai'i and Queensland, for instance) where Indians and particularly Pacific Islanders were signed up for periods of indenture in the Pacific plantations.

41   The term "pacifier" (to pacify) is a euphemism in the French colonial context for the extreme violence employed by the invaders against the indigenous peoples in order to establish colonial "order".

42   See Speedy (2006) for a discussion of these themes in "Sauvages et civilisés".

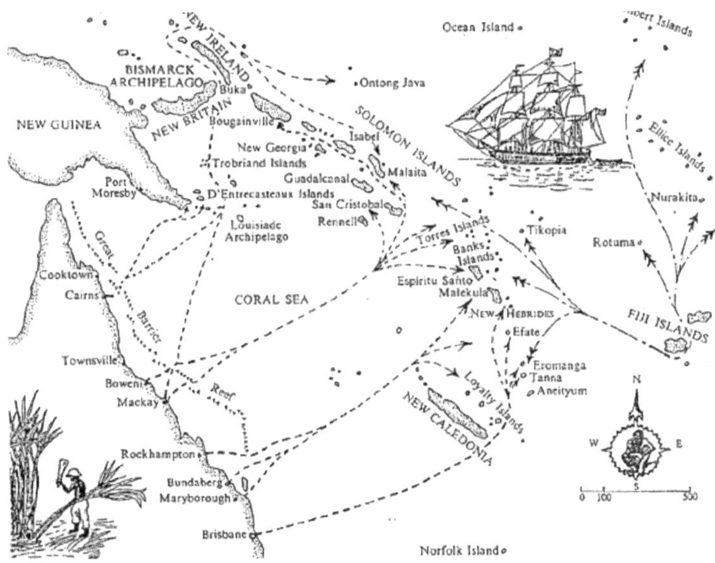

MAP 'THE MAIN RECRUITING ROUTES', P3 THE BLACKBIRDERS,
EDWARD WYBERGH DOCKER (COURTESY OF HARPERCOLLINS)

LABOUR
SCHOONER,
SYDNEY BELLE,
IN BUNDABERG,
QUEENSLAND,
1900

FRANCO-ANGLO PACIFIC CONNECTIONS — THE CASE FOR TRANSLATING "JEAN M'BARAÏ"

Set in a time before the "monolingualism of the Other" took over the Pacific, "Jean M'Baraï, the Trepang Fisherman" seems an ideal introduction to Georges Baudoux via translation for anglophone readers. Focusing on a recent, shameful chapter in Australian and Pacific history – the Pacific slave trade or Kanaka trade,[43] it describes a time when anglophone, francophone and Pacific peoples interacted, exchanged, and moved in and out of each other's lives, perhaps more frequently than today. It gives anglophone readers, Australians in particular, the opportunity to read about an episode in their history from an outsider's (although close neighbour's) perspective. As we see in "Jean M'Baraï", the transactions that took place between peoples in the frontier spaces of New Caledonia, the New Hebrides (now Vanuatu) and Australia were not based on any notions of equality. Indeed, rooted in colonial power relations and concerned with monetary gain and exploitation, they were often extremely violent.

First published in 1919 in Le Messager, reworked and "polished" in 1927, republished in 1972 in Les Blancs sont venus tome 1 and republished again in a new edition of Les Blancs sont venus in 2009, "Jean M'Baraï" is a novella rather than a short story.[44] According to O'Reilly, the character M'Baraï was inspired by the lives of three real individuals who Baudoux had known in the bush: Jules Loyau from Yandé Island, off the north western coast of New Caledonia, Louis M'Baraï, also known as Jean-Marie, who disappeared in the Diahot river near Pam in northern New Caledonia, and Dick Mackam, who had been taken to Australia by Mr Atkinson to box (O'Reilly 1950, 195).

Given its early publication date and the fact that details of the story were based on the oral histories of Baudoux's ni-Vanuatu mining employees (O'Reilly 1950, 196), themselves former Queensland Kanaka workers, "Jean M'Baraï" offers a unique window into historical debates on the nature of the Pacific labour trade. This translation into English, therefore, will be of real interest to Pacific and Labour historians for the descriptions of the recruitment of the workers, conditions on board the ships, Anglo-French competition, tensions in the Pacific over the engagement of labourers, daily life in Queensland for both new recruits and "time expired" workers, and the repatriation of the labourers at the end of their indenture.

---

43   Melanesians from Vanuatu, the Solomon Islands, New Caledonia, the Gilbert Islands, Fiji and parts of Papua New Guinea were transported to Australia as cheap indentured labour for the Queensland sugar plantations. Some 62,475 "Kanakas", as the Melanesians were called at the time, were "recruited" between 1863 and 1904. Many of these workers did not go willingly, at least in the early days of the labour trade (see, for instance, Munro 1995). A similar trade into New Caledonia occurred around the same time, and French and English slavers became competitors in the Melanesian archipelagos. See Shineberg (1999) for details on the New Caledonian Pacific labour trade. See also Speedy (2015a) for the story of the first cross-imperial blackbirding operation in 1857. See the Recommended Reading section for general references to the Pacific Labour Trade.

44   I have translated the 1972 edition of "Jean M'Baraï".

SOUTH SEA ISLANDERS ON A LABOUR VESSEL, CA 1900

SOUTH SEA ISLANDERS ARRIVING BY SHIP IN BUNDABERG, QUEENSLAND, CA 1900

COUNTRY AROUND
HAMBLEDON
SUGAR PLANTATION
NEAR CAIRNS,
QUEENSLAND,
CA 1891

(L) SOUTH SEA ISLANDER LABOURERS CLEARING LAND AT FARNBOROUGH,
QUEENSLAND, CA 1895

(R) SOUTH SEA ISLANDERS CUTTING SUGAR CANE ON A PLANTATION AT BINGERA,
QUEENSLAND, CA 1905

There is a degree of discord between academic assessment, oral histories and popular conceptions of the Pacific labour trade as a form of slavery. While Europeans had been hiring Pacific Islanders from the late 18th century for whaling and in the sandalwood, bêche-de-mer and copra trades (Shineberg, 1967), this recruitment was not commodified until the development in the second half of the 19th century of the highly labour-intensive cotton and sugar industries. Academic literature on the Pacific labour trade is divided on the extent to which blackbirding – kidnapping through violence or trickery – was a feature of recruitment.

In the late 1960s and 1970s the revisionist 'Canberra school' shifted away from the imperial history focus that had characterised earlier scholarship in order to emphasise the agency of the indentured workers (Moore 1992, Munro 1995). Hunt and Kennedy (2006, 806) have noted a swing back in the popular media to reporting the entire period of this

Pacific labour trade as being akin to 'slavery', a perspective from which the trade had been conceptualised from its beginnings (Mortenson 2000). This trend intensified in the lead-up to the 150 year anniversary of the trade in 2013 and there have been calls for apologies from the Australian government for its role in the exploitation of the Kanaka workers (see, for instance, Armbruster 2013, Ingram 2013). This view is also apparent in oral histories that have been recorded in resources such as the 1995 documentary film Sugar Slaves or dramatised as in Amie Batalibasi's short film Blackbird that is currently in production.[45] These memorialising projects serve to draw public attention to the horrors, injustices and racism suffered by the men, women and children taken from their island homes to work in the Queensland plantations.[46]

SKETCH SHOWING THE RECRUITMENT OF SOUTH SEA ISLANDERS IN NEW HEBRIDES, 1892

SOUTH SEA ISLANDERS WITH WAGONS LOADED WITH SUGAR CANE IN MACKAY, QUEENSLAND, 1895

---

45   Blackbird is yet to be released but there is a Facebook page for the project that can be consulted here: https://www.facebook.com/blackbirdfilmproject. Oral histories are also, of course, used in academic research.

46   An important feature of Shineberg's (1999) work on the indentured workers taken to New Caledonia was the vivid picture of their lives that she was able to draw through meticulous archival research.

SOUTH SEA ISLANDER LABOURERS LOADING SUGAR CANE ON TRAIN WAGONS AT BINGERA, QUEENSLAND, CA 1898

HAMBLEDON SUGAR MILL NEAR CAIRNS, QUEENSLAND, CA 1895

Whether or not blackbirding continued for the duration of the labour trade, there is agreement among academics and descendants of the workers that, at least in the early days, coercion was widespread. "Voluntarism", cautions Doug Hunt, "should not be over-emphasised. Most historians recognise that, among Islanders, the degree of informed consent and individual willingness to enlist varied considerably. The consensus is that instances of deception, trickery and violence did take place, especially in the early years of the trade" (Hunt 2007, 38-39). More recently, Tracey Banivanua-Mar has argued:

[t]hroughout the life of the trade, a lack of consent from individual Islanders rarely stood in the way of recruiters' profits, and while not always overt and ever-present in labor recruiters' behavior, violence and aggression continued to underpin the viability of colonial trades in the western Pacific (Banivanua-Mar 2007, 27).

Baudoux's story would seem to support this conclusion.

AN OVERSEER'S HOUSE, HAMBLEDON SUGAR PLANTATION, CAIRNS, QUEENSLAND, CA 1891

LOG HUTS USED BY AUSTRALIAN SOUTH SEA ISLANDER LABOURERS ON A SUGAR PLANTATION IN QUEENSLAND, 1907

SOUTH SEA ISLANDER HUTS AT WATAWA PLANTATION NEAR BUNDABERG, QUEENSLAND, CA 1897

SOUTH SEA ISLANDER LABOURERS LEAVING TRAIN CARRIAGES AT INNISFAIL, QUEENSLAND TO EMBARK ON THE JOURNEY BACK TO THE ISLAND WHERE THEY WERE RECRUITED, CA 1902

In "Jean M'Baraï", Baudoux is at his ambivalent best. On the one hand, the colonial, racist stereotypes are out in full force, on the other, his critique of colonisation and civilisation is also compellingly made through his frank descriptions of the exploitation of the Other at the hands of the "savage" civilised. It is a story full of contradictions and paradoxes and although its tone and content might seem overtly racist to the contemporary reader, they serve as stark reminders of the discourses that have shaped modern Australia and New Caledonia.

"Jean M'Baraï" traces the eventful life of a métis, a half-caste, born to a seafaring Breton adventurer and a Melanesian woman from Poya in New Caledonia, who had been bought from her tribe in exchange for cooking pots, wool and tobacco. Jean M'Baraï, the "strong, handsome" child of "early colonisation", whose birth is unregistered (thus illegitimate in the eyes of the Administration)[47] is a perfect vehicle for Baudoux to explore the theories of heredity that so fascinated him, to meditate on the role of "genealogy, kinship, lineage and breeding in the transmission of characteristics", while also discussing the way one's upbringing and environment can shape a person's development (Speedy 2013a). Indeed, in this story, conflicting colonial discourses surrounding the half-caste, whether his body and mind represent a site of "degeneration" or "regeneration", are debated (Speedy 2013a). Is the half-caste a monstrous being, more savage than civilised? Or is he the symbol of hope for the "degraded" colonised race, a sign that through crossbreeding, the savage can become civilised? In which world (white or black) does he belong?

Throughout the story, Baudoux portrays the animalised body of Jean M'Baraï as a commodity destined for capture, exploitation and consumption by both black and white society.[48] While physical incarceration features in the narrative, it is more M'Baraï's metaphorical imprisonment in both the "savage" and "civilised" worlds that prevents him from living fully in either.

Baudoux contrives that his genetic makeup dictates the limited roles he can play in either world. Despite his best efforts and masterful performance (through costume and speech, shrewd planning and intense physical exertion), M'Baraï remains ostracised, not recognised as belonging by the members of these two opposing worlds. He sits at the crossroads, occupying an in-between or liminal space. Although, according to colonial lore, the *métis* had the potential for both degeneration and regeneration, M'Baraï demonstrates neither.

[B]y giving M'Baraï many of the hallmarks of a monster, [Baudoux] also shows that the racist views of society (both white and black) exclude the *métis* from belonging anywhere. His hybrid person, representing the taboo of miscegenation, threatens the borders of identity of both communities and he is condemned to live on the margins (Speedy 2013a).

As Raylene Ramsay (2014) points out, this rejection of Otherness is a common theme too among other early New Caledonia writers such as Jean Mariotti and Alin Laubreaux whose works betray the "premise that racial or cultural Otherness is fatal to relationships and that

---

47   In New Caledonia, the term métis was used frequently to describe ethnically mixed people. It was not, however, a legal status. Whether the "half-caste" was deemed Kanak (and thus a colonial "subject" under the Indigenous Code of 1887) or a French citizen depended on whether his birth had been registered and he had been legally recognized by his (white) father.

48   Parts of this section are drawn from Speedy (2013a).

colonial society lacks the capacity to embrace diversity" (24). Ultimately, for the colonial writer, *métissage* is impossible and there is a "need to choose one's own camp" (24).

Cannibalism is used, as in much colonial literature, as a means of demonising the "primitive" Other. In *Jean M'Baraï*, cannibalism demarcates the savage from the civilised and its role appears to provide a reason or excuse for colonial violence and depravity in the guise of the 'pacification' of indigenous peoples or in their enslavement. However, Baudoux, as I have argued:

> *[. . .] also portrays the metaphoric cannibalism of indigenous peoples through colonisation by way of body commodification, exploitation and consumption, capitalist greed, land expropriation and the civilising mission. Here we have the sublime ambiguity of Baudoux - for, if the black world is savage, frightening and brutal the 'civilised' white world is no less cruel and inhumane. Jean M'Baraï thus has the dual function of presenting a critique of colonialism and civilisation while at the same time providing a vehicle for racist discourses (Speedy 2013a).*

This underlines the merit of reading Baudoux today. The dual reading that he invites both conforms to and subverts reader expectations. On the surface, the narrator of the story gives voice to the prejudices – suffused in Social Darwinist ideologies – of white settler society. In this vision of might is right, power sits squarely in the hands of the strongest who, no matter what the context – in the Malekulan bush, on board a blackbirding ship or on a sugar plantation in Australia – vanquish the weak. The losers like M'Baraï the *métis*, doomed by his weak or diluted genes, are destined for exploitation.

Separate from the narrator, Baudoux in his authorial role presents a harsh and much more honest view of "civilised" colonial society which, for him, is just as barbaric as any so-called "primitive" one. Savagery has no limits, no boundaries and is not restricted to any particular "race". As a parallel discourse, it is subversive and significant in the postcolonial flavour of its critique of the colonial project.

Would Baudoux's readers in 1919 have interpreted the story in such a way? We cannot be sure. The narrator's racist commentary seems there to "appease or comfort the colonial reader, to reassure him or her that the frank depiction of the brutality of colonialism is a just reflection of the natural order of things" (Speedy 2013a). Baudoux, a white man of privilege, but one who had also experienced life on the fringes of settler society in his various occupations in the bush, had an acute understanding of the complexity of the colonial encounter. He may have been attempting a lesson in cultural relativism, indirectly schooling his audience through the duality of his text. Or the dialogical relationship between narrator and author could stand for his inner turmoil in the face of societal inequities that he had accepted and profited from himself.

We may never know Baudoux's true agenda but he has left us with a multivocal text that both supports and subverts the binaries of savagery and civilisation and remains a testament to the relentless and conflicting imperatives of colonialism.

TRANSLATING "JEAN M'BARAÏ" — LINGUISTIC CHALLENGES

Jean M'Baraï is something of an historical emblem for people, both black and white, eking out an existence on the fringes and frontiers of colonial society. He is, in effect, caught between two worlds, yet he belongs to neither. The only place he fits in is the brousse (bush) of a certain time, a frontier space where racial and linguistic lines are blurred. Indeed, M'Baraï's hybrid language also stands for this in-between space and, when faced with the "monolingualism of the Other" of later colonisation, M'Baraï can no longer comprehend either the language or the society. In this new colonial order, which in 1904 went so far as to outlaw the métis (cf. Martin 1995a, 444), Jean M'Baraï is a displaced person. While showing certain linguistic skills, M'Baraï inadvertently wears his language as a sign of difference, which can also be a source of frustration when attempting to communicate with the (black or white) Other.

M'Baraï's language is bichelamar, a pidgin or contact language spoken throughout the Pacific. New Caledonian bichelamar was spoken by white, Polynesian and other adventurers, who plied the coasts for trade, in their interactions with local Kanak. It was initially English and Polynesian based with some input from Melanesian languages. Once the French became firmly entrenched in the colony, the pidgin slowly shifted to become more French based. M'Baraï's pidgin is essentially the pidgin of first contacts (i.e. English / Polynesian based). However, there is one example which shows a curious mixture of French, English and pidgin / creole elements: "Vous couillon ! Je apporté à vous un l'ancre, un chaîne. This morning vous pas look clouds partir straight Arama to go Belep, comme barrière, imouang."[49] Whether this represents language change - the movement from the English to French based Melanesian pidgin - or whether it is simply an idiosyncrasy is debateable.

As with Baudoux's representations of other languages and idioms of the New Caledonian bush, his reproduction of bichelamar (spoken by M'Baraï, some of the Kanak of Malekula, the Kanak labourers in Queensland and New Caledonian half-caste Louis Laurent) is imperfect. While it generally looks like a good representation of pidgin, there are a few syntactical errors. In this example, "House here belong you", it would be more usual to see "House belong you here". In "Think you finish dead long time?", "finish" should follow "dead" and "Yes, me go now, ground here finish belong me" ought to be something more like "Yes, me go now, ground belong me finish".[50]

When it came to translating the varieties of bichelamar in the text, then, I needed to consider their purpose in the story and their historical importance for all peoples of the Pacific. Jean M'Baraï's bichelamar, for instance, reflects his mixed ethnic and cultural identity and

---

49   You idiot! I brought you an anchor and a chain. This morning you didn't look at the clouds and went straight to Arama to go to Belep, like a reef, bad.

50   Renowned creolist and specialist on Pacific Pidgins, Philip Baker, pointed out these syntactical errors (personal communication 24/09/2012). Baker put forward the argument that New South Wales Pidgin, a language that developed from early Aboriginal and British settler contacts in Sydney but that spread throughout New South Wales and up to Queensland, formed an important input in the development of Melanesian Pidgin English (Baker 1993). See Jakelin Troy's (1994) doctoral thesis for a more information on this contact language and for a recent overview of contact languages in Australia see Meakins (2014).

the bichelamar spoken by the Kanak in Malekula and Queensland denotes their status as victims of blackbirding. The bichelamar also reminds readers "of a time when hybrid varieties of English, French and Pacific languages could be heard throughout the region and that these mixed voices were vehicles of communication rather than communication barriers" (Speedy 2015b).

With an overarching, although not exclusively, "foreignising" (cf. Venuti 1998) translation strategy, opting to preserve as much as possible the historical, cultural and linguistic specificities of Baudoux's 19th century world, I have chosen not to translate the examples of bichelamar in "Jean M'Baraï".[51] I leave them in the English text exactly as they appear in the French text, errors and all. Indeed, echoing Baudoux's decision not to gloss[52] the mixed French / English example for his French-speaking readers but offering a gloss in a footnote for the English-based utterances of the Malekulan Kanak, I have provided a gloss only for the example containing French for my anglophone readers, trusting that they will be able to work out the general idea of the English-based pidgin samples. In this way, I attempt to recreate a similar effect on English-speaking readers as the one Baudoux's French readers would have had – that of almost understanding but not quite, and of recognizing the otherness and hybridity of this language from another time.[53] My choice to keep the bichelamar as Baudoux wrote it is also driven by my belief that these fragments of bichelamar from New Caledonia, Vanuatu and Queensland are of historical and linguistic interest for readers. Retaining them thus provides anglophone readers and researchers access to Baudoux's literary representations of these 19th century Pacific contact languages.

When translating "Jean M'Baraï", I was mindful that much of the racist language and racial stereotypes would shock the 21st century reader. Yet, they are an integral part of the rough, violent and deeply racist worldviews of the characters in Baudoux's story. Changing them would not only betray the writer's style, but would dilute his message, misrepresenting him and the historical era about which he is writing. The word "nigger" was, for instance, the only reasonable option to translate the French nègre.[54] Baudoux borrows heavily from the language of the slave trade to describe the Kanaka trade (as did the trade itself) and even uses the English forms "nigga" and "nigger" numerous times himself in the French text. This reflects anglophone usage of the time. Indeed in 19th century Queensland, Kanak workers were referred to as "niggers" in both historical documents and literature from the period. Similarly, the term "half-caste", which is now outdated, was the equivalent of métis in the English-speaking Pacific as was "Chinaman" for le chinois.

---

51   My aim to maintain the integrity of the nineteenth century world that Baudoux portrays, particularly in terms of the language varieties, languages and cultural references in his text, means that I generally adopt a foreignising translation strategy. However, as Ramsay and Walker (2010, 47) have pointed out with regards to the translation of indigenous writing, a wholly uncritical foreignising approach is not always desirable as it can lead to stilted prose and an "obscure and overly literal" translation that exoticises in a "patronising and/or elitist manner". While I have, then, avoided "spoonfeeding" the reader through excessive exegesis, my translation does, at times, adopt some domestication, particularly in terms of ensuring readability. This critical introduction, of course, allows me to act as cultural mediator by contextualising the work and explaining crucial elements of the text to the reader unfamiliar with the history of the Pacific region. The Recommended Reading section following the Bibliography also gives readers a list of resources for further information.

52   Offer a brief or literal translation or explanation.

53   While this decision allows for a reasonably similar effect, Baudoux's readers were of course much closer (in time and space) to these contact languages.

54   Nègre is a pejorative term, which can be translated as "Negro", "slave" or "nigger".

"THE KANAKA AT HOME."

"JUST LANDED."

"THREE YEARS AFTER."

ABOVE: A THREE PART CARTOON SERIES DEPICTING THE PROGRESSION OF SOUTH SEA ISLANDER LABOURERS IN AUSTRALIA, PUBLISHED IN THE GRAPHIC, A BRITISH WEEKLY ILLUSTRATED NEWSPAPER, LONDON, ENGLAND, 1882.

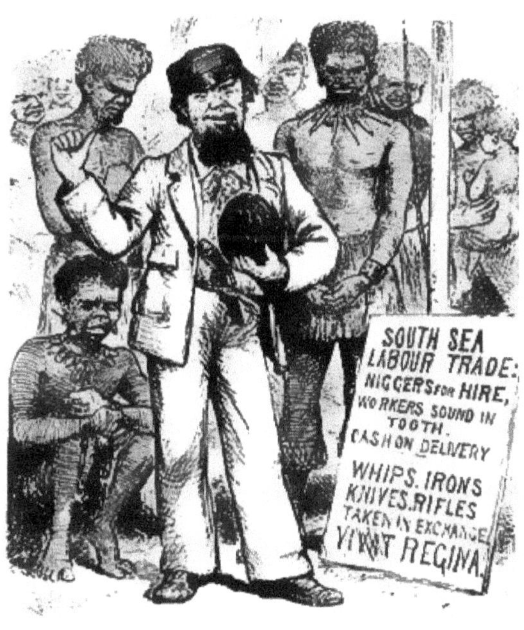

SOUTH SEA LABOUR TRADE, A CARTOON FROM "THE BULLETIN" (AN AUSTRALIAN NEWSPAPER), C1886

"SOUTH SEA ISLAND TRADER: 'NOW GENTLEMEN, GIVE ME A START. WHAT SHALL WE SAY FOR THIS 'ERE COCOANUT – AND THE NIGGER THROWN IN? FIVE POUNDS ONLY BID FOR THIS COCOANUT. FIVE POUNDS; FIVE O'NY; FIVE – DID I HEAR SIX? NO ADVANCE; GOING AT FIVE; GONE. NEXT NIGGER; I MEAN NEXT COCOANUT.' "

The term "Kanak" itself is interesting. Once a pejorative colonial name for the indigenous people of New Caledonia, it has been reclaimed by the Melanesian population and adopted as the official term to designate their group. They have eschewed the variable French spelling (canaque(s)) in favour of the invariable Kanak. While I use this recent, invariable form in this introduction, it would be anachronistic to do so in the translated text. Baudoux, naturally, uses canaque(s), and I have substituted this with the English spelling "Kanak" but have made the noun variable to echo the usage of the time. Baudoux does not differentiate between the "canaques" of New Caledonia and the "canaques" of the New Hebrides (present-day Vanuatu). However, the Melanesians who were victims of blackbirding in the 19th century and who were sent to work principally in Queensland or Fiji, were known in English as Kanakas. I have therefore chosen to use this term in my translation when Baudoux is specifically referring to Melanesians taken in this trade.[55] When he is simply referring to the indigenous inhabitants of New Caledonia or the New Hebrides (Vanuatu), I retain the term Kanak in its variable form.

In keeping with my desire not to overly domesticate the translation, Kanak and pidgin words in Baudoux's text ("popinée", "pilou", "takata" etc.) have been retained in the translation, maintaining the local flavour in the translated text.

Finally, Baudoux frequently uses English vocabulary in the French text. Some of these words are used in the New Caledonian context. A few entered New Caledonian French via bichelamar. Most English words, however, were imported by Australian stockmen who settled in New Caledonia in the 19th century to set up cattle stations. Baudoux also uses a number of English words and phrases when describing the action in Queensland. Interestingly, none of these examples are glossed, indicating that Baudoux's readers would have been unfazed by the juxtaposition of the two languages, perhaps reminding them of the not too distant past when varieties of English were heard more often in the colony. While there is no way this effect can be reproduced in the translation (as it is all in English), I have chosen to italicise English words used by Baudoux to give the anglophone reader an idea of the extent to which he peppered his French text with English.

"Jean M'Baraï" is a fascinating story from both a historical and linguistic perspective. Raw, brutal, and confronting, it has been exciting and somewhat challenging to translate. I hope I have managed to do Baudoux justice and let the 19th century voice of Jean M'Baraï, the half-caste New Caledonian blackbirder / blackbird, cross the postcolonial "linguistic divide" to resonate with 21st century English-speaking readers in the Pacific and beyond.

---

55   It should be noted that Kanaka is today seen as a racist slur among descendants of the Pacific Islanders who have made their homes in Australia. The preferred appellation is South Sea Islander.

ACKNOWLEDGEMENTS

This project was funded by a Macquarie University Research Development Grant (2010-2012), Grant Reference Number: 9201000826.

I would like to thank Professor Gabriel Valet of the *Société d'Études Historiques de la Nouvelle-Calédonie* for granting me permission to translate and publish the 1972 edition of *Jean M'Baraï le pêcheur de tripangs*. My thanks also to Bernard Gasser and Eddy Banaré for permitting me to reproduce images of Georges Baudoux and his family, and to Véronique Fillol for her wonderful collegiality.

I dedicate this literary baby to my daughters Aliyah and Shahrazad.

GEORGES BAUDOUX'S
jean m'baraï
THE trepang
fisherman

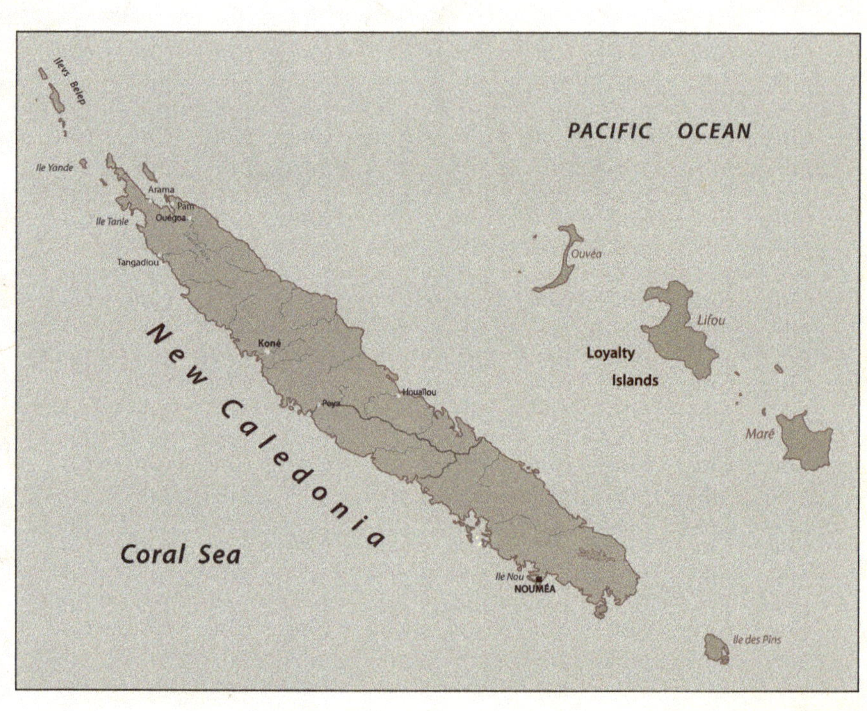

Îlevs Belep
Île Yande
Arama
Parr
Ouégoa
Île Tanle
Tangadiou
Koné
Poya
Houaïlou
New Caledonia
Coral Sea
Île Nou
NOUMÉA
PACIFIC OCEAN
Ouvéa
Lifou
Loyalty
Islands
Maré
Île des Pins

INTRODUCTION

You didn't know my friend M'Baraï… Jean M'Baraï, did you? I bet his name means nothing to you… I really miss him, you know – he was a good lad.

I met him, many years ago now, on a fishing expedition for bêche-de-mer. We'd often meet on the reefs and sand cays. Driven by the need for solidarity that brings folk who live off the sea and fishermen together, it was quite natural that we helped each other out. He'd give me some of his yams, I'd share my bread with him. When he had crayfish, he'd always put a few aside for me. And I'd bring him rum and wine when I came back from getting supplies.

As I was new to the job, he showed me the best fishing spots and told me the most favourable times to fish. He taught me coastal navigation and where best to seek shelter. He schooled me in predicting the direction of the wind and forecasting bad weather. Like the seabirds, Jean M'Baraï knew instinctively how to read the great outdoors. The thoroughness of his observations amazed me – the shapes of the clouds, their different movements, the colour of the faraway mountains seen through the mist, the hue of the sky reflected by the sea, the flocks of gulls heading back to the islands, the schools of fish swimming by, the sea rumbling on the reefs at night, the phases of the moon, the tides - all those little things that escape the uninitiated were for him almost infallible meteorological signs.

One day out fishing, I was caught off guard by some bad weather blowing in from the north east. I was imprisoned in a lagoon in the great reef and there was no escape. At low tide it was okay – I was surrounded by a coral enclosure. It was like I was in a little lake – the water was pretty calm. But, at high tide, it was no joke – the swells broke from all sides, rolling violently over the reefs to come crashing together in the lagoon where they rose up in a tremendous tidal bore. It was impossible to cross back over the coral plateau where I had entered the lagoon. Now and then, between swells, the water subsided and the plateau was temporarily exposed. If I had tried to go back that way though, the boat would have been smashed to smithereens.

The anchor was hooked securely into the rocks but at times the cutter pitched, reared up and pulled so sharply on the chain that each time I thought I could feel it breaking away. Then the wave would bury itself under the bow, the boat would lurch and seem to fall into nothingness. And then the same process would begin over again, each time more frightening than the last.

The night was black, the wind whistled in through the ship's rigging and sails, the rain whipped everything in its way and the tide was rising again. If the chain broke, the boat would be thrown in an instant onto the reefs that were just behind the stern then under the giant columns of luminous water that broke formidably over each other, spraying up foam that the wind propelled away. The boat, the three Kanaks on board and I were going to be rolled over and crushed like the insignificant little things we were. And there was nothing we could do except count on the chain being strong enough… and, at that point, it seemed as flimsy as hell.

So there I was, weighing up my chances, protecting myself as best I could from the rain pelting my boat's rickety deck. Suddenly, a violent thud shook the hull. I thought that the boat had just hit a rock. I jumped on the deck. A little craft was cavorting chaotically alongside and a man, clinging to the mast stays of my cutter, was securing a mooring rope. I approached him and in the squall and driving rain he shouted, "Vous couillon ! Je apporté à vous un l'ancre, un chaîne. This morning vous pas look clouds partir straight Arama to go Belep, comme barrière, imouang."[56] He burst out laughing as he gave me a friendly whack before gripping my shoulder. With this gesture, it seemed as though he was taking possession of my person, a prize that he had wrangled off the elements.

It was my mate M'Baraï who, worried about what had become of me, had set two reefs in his sail and had cruised through the night, windward of the lagoon, where I was in a bad way. Then, at high tide, without worrying that he might drown, he'd jumped in his *dinghy* and, letting himself be carried along by the wind and the swell, negotiating the waves head-on and surfing in on the foamy white rollers, he traversed the middle reef that closed off the lagoon. And he did all this to help me out, to bring me his anchor and his chain.

In the meantime, his boat, which was about five tons, was being driven by his popinée and two Kanaks.[57] It continued on its way, hugging the wind, to go up near Tangadiou where it would most likely run aground or moor itself in some creek full of mangroves as it no longer had its anchor.

We cast the second anchor, mooring across the first to create a V shape, making sure that the chains were of equal length, and we were safe. M'Baraï was dripping wet. I gave him a change of clothes but he would only accept a coat so as not to be naked in front of me as he took off his pants. To seal our friendship and to warm ourselves up, we polished off an old bottle of rum.

I don't know whether my cutter's chain would have continued to hold against the repeated violent jolts of the waves but if it didn't, and I fear it wouldn't have, I believe good old M'Baraï saved my life. And if not, his intention equalled the deed. Whatever the case, I was very happy when he turned up, bringing with him the salvation of his sheet anchor and the comfort of his experience.

The following afternoon, the wind and the sea having calmed down somewhat, M'Baraï, who knew all the passages and could judge at a glance the water's depths, piloted the cutter. He made it snake through the water over the coral and, at half-tide, managed to get it out of the lagoon where it had been imprisoned.

So that was how I got to know my friend, M'Baraï. As you can see, we weren't introduced in a drawing room. The least you could say is that our relationship was not conventional.

But I haven't yet told you M'Baraï's story. I haven't told you about his very eventful life, a life full of adventures, even if he was quite an uncomplicated soul. His story seemed interesting to me as it encapsulates that of a certain type of character – characters who are quite widespread in the islands of Oceania but are nonetheless not well known.

---

56   Gloss: You idiot! I brought you an anchor and a chain. This morning you didn't look at the clouds and went straight to Arama to go to Belep, like a reef, bad.

57   "Popinée" was a term used to refer to Kanak women in colonial New Caledonia.

PART ONE

M'Baraï was a stocky half-caste with short legs - he was unusually broad, built like a bull and as strong as one too. Out of vanity, he wore little gold hoops in his ears. M'Baraï had been conceived on a boat and born on a boat. He was a very good boy, a devoted friend, not someone who picked fights – though he would take on any that came his way with a certain amount of pleasure. Unfortunately, he was a bit simple, very stubborn and for good reason.

His father was a true Breton who spoke Breton and kept up his Breton traditions. He was a topman in the sailing ships, a seaman who was discharged in New Caledonia in about 1859. He went into business for himself, trading along the coast, fishing for trepang, cutting sandalwood and bartering with the Kanaks.

One fine day our Breton felt the need to get married and not having a wimple-wearing Breton lady handy – a bit hopeful there my fellow – bought a superb popinée from the Kanaks at Poya. He paid for her with a huge cast-iron cooking pot and a three-legged cauldron. To seal the deal he had to add six skeins of red wool and forty sticks of tobacco. In return for this sum and no other formality, he had a very happy household, or so said the old men up North who knew what they were talking about as they also partook in these sorts of unofficial marriages.

My friend Jean M'Baraï was born from this union between a Celt and a Melanesian from the tribe of the Ounouas.[58] As there was no registrar of births on the coast back then, his father didn't register him – besides, he didn't care, his son was his, he knew it and it was nobody else's business – Oh yes indeed – he didn't need a piece of paper to prove it. And in Brittany it was the priest's job to take care of all that…

Now that he had a wife and child, the sailor settled definitively in the country. He got a plot of land in the North – there were a few coconut palms growing on it. It was situated in a bay battered by waves and at the foot of sheer rocks and cliffs that must have reminded him of Amorique in his native Brittany. There he built a *home*, continued to sail through force

---

58 The "Ounouas", as the French called them, were in fact the Ûrûwë clan (cf. Bensa and Leblic, 2000, 25) who originally came from Ponérihouen but resettled in Pouembout well before European colonisation.

of habit and started off by gathering copra and planting coconut palms.

His son Jean M'Baraï, who he called "his sailor", grew in strength and skill. At four he could swim like a fish and was already spear fishing. All the little Kanaks of the neighbouring tribe, the pikininis, were his competitors in sport and his friends. At ten, he could row for hours, he knew how to sail a yacht and he could bring down coconuts with his slingshot… At eighteen, he was a strong and healthy young man, confident and very modest – a true Breton cast in bronze. He got his excellent sailing skills and his love for the big blue from his father. From his mother, he inherited the gifts of dexterity and flexibility and his tremendous talent at diving. Yet, while his physique had developed, his mind remained uncultured. He couldn't read or count and he spoke mainly either bichelamar or Kanak. He hardly ever spoke his father's Breton-accented French. He had already had many successes with the beautiful girls of the local tribes. He always won fights when the prize was a black temptress.

Around this time, his father decided that the little coastal shipping route around New Caledonia was not extensive enough to make his son a real sailor. For this reason (and also to calm his raging hormones), he launched him into open-sea navigation.

Bemoaning the fact that Jean could be neither a Newfoundland fisherman nor a whaler, and in order to make him a coastal captain, he sent him off to sail with one of his friends, something of a pirate captain who prowled the archipelagos in his schooner, recruiting black New Hebrideans to sell elsewhere.

Jean M'Baraï was very happy to board a big ship, to embark upon a life of adventure. His home port was Noumea. He went on two campaigns of about six months each and each time he returned home enthused.

Just imagine! We gathered up Kanakas and popinées as if we were hunting or fishing. When they didn't want to come willingly, we took them by surprise, tricked them or resorted to violence. Often, some of them would defend themselves by shooting at us. In the name of "might makes right", we'd use the women, in their natural role, before selling them, taking our turn according to hierarchy – the captain going first and so on down the ranks. A black man's life wasn't worth much unless he was merchandise safely stored at the bottom of the hold. We could kill one to test a rifle's range or to prove him guilty.

Sometimes a whole lot of us would go ashore silently and well-armed to boot. We'd surround a village and take prisoners. If we didn't succeed, we'd take pot shots at runaways and burn down huts in retaliation. We'd break everything, stealing copra, pigs or anything of value.

Some nights, depending on the circumstances, we'd prepare a whaleboat and hide it near the coast, behind a headland or in a cove, so its occupants could keep watch over the dugout canoes. So as to reassure the very suspicious islanders, the schooner would make a conspicuous departure, heading towards the open sea. At daybreak, a few small canoes would unsuspectingly set off from the shore. The men were going fishing and their sole focus was the fish. At an opportune moment, the whaleboat would shoot out towards them, oars going at full pace, cutting them off from any retreat and keeping them there at gunpoint. When the Kanakas realised they were trapped, they'd jump in the water, diving under, scattering and trying to swim away – it was every man for himself. It was then that the real fishing began - and it was really entertaining. We'd fish out the divers with boathooks while the powerful Loyalty Islanders from the whaleboat jumped into the sea and had swimming races to catch the escapees. There were Homeric struggles in the water but the swimmers from the slave ship, supported by the well-armed boat, always overcame their stunned prey. During these nigger-fishing jaunts, you'd often get a few of them making it to shore and as punishment we'd shoot at them.

Should a French or English warship be spotted patrolling the islands, the schooner would trade honestly, exchanging goods and only recruiting Kanakas who were willing to go. When the cargo was too compromising, the schooner made its escape, at full sail, going far into unexplored territory, into supposedly inaccessible parts of the archipelago.

It was a way of life that suited Jean M'Baraï to a tee, for the atavistic instincts of a Breton privateer and a Kanak warrior were lying dormant in him, waiting only to be awoken. Spurred on by his pirate captain, he found these brutal and inhumane practices quite in keeping with the Laws of Nature.

The schooner left for a third expedition with Jean M'Baraï listed as bosun. It returned after several months at sea but Jean M'Baraï was no longer aboard. In the logbook he was reported missing at sea, having disappeared one night with a small craft. It was impossible to get any more information.

His father lamented his disappearance as much as was necessary. Then he stoically accepted the fact that his son had died a sailor, that the sea had eaten him up as it had done to many other family members. He was powerless to do anything … since it was the spirits of the dead who called sailors into the sea and into their watery graves.

The old settler's property was in yield - the coconut trees he had planted were enough for his modest existence. He sailed for pleasure only, pushed by the desire to be drenched in sea spray, a desire that all old seamen harbour forever.

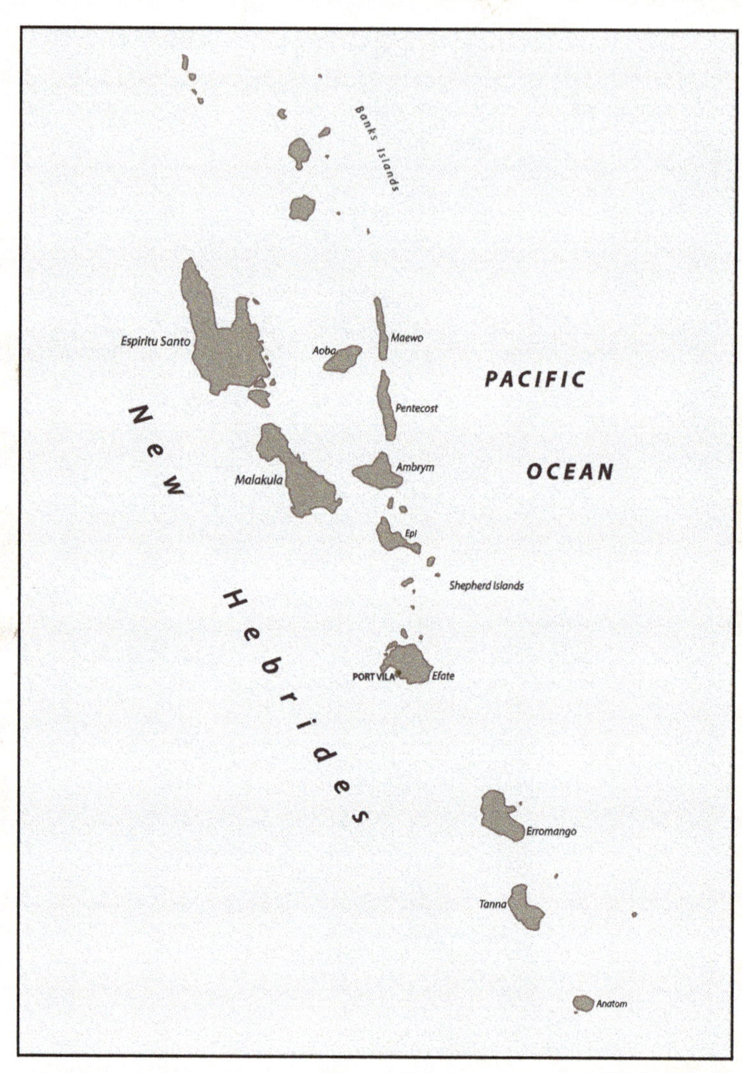

Banks Islands
Espiritu Santo
Aoba
Maewo
PACIFIC
Pentecost
New
OCEAN
Ambrym
Malakula
Epi
Shepherd Islands
Hebrides
PORT VILA
Efate
Erromango
Tanna
Anatom

PART TWO

I

The schooner cruised around the New Hebrides archipelago and recruitment was going well for the slave traders. Indeed, the campaign was promising to be rather fruitful.

The recruiters had had a bit of good luck on Santo. Several tribes were at war, bent on genocide. After bloody conflicts and much gorging of human flesh, the defeated, or the deserters, had come to the boat themselves, wanting to be taken aboard. They were strong healthy men who were worth at least twenty-five pounds sterling a head.

On Aoba Island, a rather fortunate roundup had filled a small boat. The best of the haul were five popinées. Aoba girls were highly valued by connoisseurs.

This race looks more or less Polynesian. There was a history of crossbreeding which seemed due to migrations from the Wallis Islands. The natives no longer remembered. The people are saffron-coloured with rather fine features and bright eyes. Throughout their short-lived youth, the women's bodies are supple, graceful and pleasing to look at. Knowing that they are beautiful, it is vanity that impels the girls to use leaves to hide their genitals and decorate themselves with lianas and seashells. As this feminine merchandise was top of the line, there was always competition among buyers.

In other islands, recruitment was somewhat haphazard. Nonetheless, there were already sixty or so men (who owed nothing to anyone) packed together in the hold. And this was without the women. So as not to expose them to the lechery of the sequestered Kanakas and to cater to the needs of the crew, the women had been kept aside.

A few rare Europeans, daredevils, bolstered by the strength of their companions - Kanaks from other lands - had settled temporarily on certain islands where the natives were not so ferocious. Trade with them had provided copra, sandalwood and mother of pearl. Some of the cheap trade goods had gone. For the ship owner, who was also the captain, everything was going well. Served by divine Providence, he led a happy life, drinking brandy with his black mistresses.

The schooner had been plying its particular trade on the coasts of Pentecost Island for a week.

In those days of early colonisation, most seamen who navigated around the Melanesian archipelagos were adventurers, crazy men from all over the world and from all sorts of provenances. These rugged characters, spurred both by money and an inherent bad streak, encouraged further by a succession of unpunished crimes, by habit and as much for their well being as for the suffering of others, progressively and by emulation came to form a mentality that was very much their own. Any sense of right and wrong had been destroyed by their desire for riches and an easy life, not to mention their depravity. Piracy, pillage and murder were recognised as necessary institutions, looked upon with indifference by those who were not directly involved. Kanakas were animals created purely for their profit or their pleasure. When they prowled around the labyrinths of the archipelagos, far from the reaches of civilisation, these white men became barbarians. The only laws known to them were vigour, nerve and brute strength.

The crews of these 150-ton schooners were partly made up of Loyalty Islanders. The rest consisted of Kanaks from other islands who had proved their loyalty to the captain, having shown cunning and verve in catching their fellow islanders.

On board, discipline was brutal for everything that had to do with the ship's operation, but it was totally relaxed when it came to morals. To ensure that the men stayed on as recruiters, quite a dangerous job at times, they needed to be encouraged in a positive, immediate and inexpensive way. So they were allowed to reward themselves in kind, taking care not to damage the female merchandise.

As the bosun, Jean M'Baraï was classed fourth, after the supercargo, in the shipboard hierarchy. He wasn't able to enter the officers' cabin but his rank afforded him some material benefits. Under the command of the captain and the first mate, coarse despotic blokes who, for him, represented all discretionary power, all human knowledge and the height of civilisation, Jean M'Baraï had become, without even realising it, a total brute. On their behalf, he was quick with his fists and very often he would use a knotted rope to make those in his charge obey him more smartly. There were probably a few black sailors with zebra-striped backs who held a grudge against him.

When it came to the lot of popinées, M'Baraï was fourth to have dibs on the merchandise. He made full use of this undisputed privilege that had become the custom. He had chosen a young woman from Aoba who, despite her resistance, had become by force "Madame M'Baraï", temporarily at least. Their union, which was initially imposed by violence, had lasted several weeks and, in spite of everything, the brutish M'Baraï had become more human through his relationship with this popinée on whom he lavished his attention and care. What is more, he had now become jealous, keeping her under close surveillance. She belonged to him.

This same young popinée whose physical appearance was pleasing to those individuals who only knew that kind of beauty, was also coveted by some of the black sailors who hung around her whenever they could. Having seen what they were up to, M'Baraï had whipped a few of them with his knotted rope. Yet the same thing happened on several occasions. Things continued on in this vein without, however, troubling other shipboard business.

II

The sky was clear with only a few fluffy white clouds floating up high. A little southeasterly breeze was blowing in. Since sunset the schooner had been sailing towards Ambrym Island. From Pentecost, she was heading south south west. As the weather was beautiful and the next day they would arrive at their destination, the last small boat to come in from shore had not been hoisted to the davit. It was still being towed behind. And the slave ship, with the wind full in her sails, sailed merrily on.

The tropical night reflected her stars in the Ocean. Jean M'Baraï was on watch, a Loyalty Islander at the helm steered the ship and three Kanak sailors, sprawled lazily on the deck, were waiting for the moment when they could make themselves useful. Next to the large open hatch, from where emanated the hot, acrid stench of the human livestock cooped up at the bottom of the hold, two Kanaks armed with Schneider shotguns were standing guard.

The hatch was only closed during storms. The rest of the time, it was left wide open to let the air circulate around the live cargo. The nigger stock couldn't be left to suffocate or die from some dirty disease spawned from its greasy stink or excrement. That would have been a dead loss valued in advance in pounds sterling.

For five or six days the ship had been on the same tack without having to execute a manoeuvre. The men on watch were half asleep and lying about on deck. Jean M'Baraï had already filled and smoked his pipe numerous times, thinking of very little. He mostly looked over at a certain deckhouse where the popinées who were not otherwise occupied were crammed in. His popinée was among them. Apart from the sound of the sea lapping the length of the hull and the wind whistling gently through the rigging, there wasn't a sound on board. Everyone was sleeping.

The wind freshened, the swell, impeded by a random current, was becoming rougher, more jarring, and the schooner went increasingly faster on her course.

M'Baraï worried about the whaleboat that was still being towed - its painter was not the strongest and he thought it might break. He gave orders to the men on watch who went immediately to grab a hawser to double the strength of the towrope. Then the schooner veered windward to slow down and thus allow the three Kanaks to pull on the whaleboat's painter to bring it alongside the ship. When the whaleboat was within reach, M'Baraï, who could only rely on himself to do a good job, jumped in, intent on threading the towrope through the anchor ring and tying it to one of the seats.

Once inside, out of habit and so they wouldn't get in his way, he put the oars back where they belonged, attaching them to the bench seats. They had been knocked out of place by the rolling waves. While he was busy doing this short task, he failed to notice that the whaleboat was moving away from the schooner, only following it very slowly. When he looked up to ask for the end of the hawser, the whaleboat was no longer moving while the schooner continued on her course. He shouted out orders that were carried away on the wind…

And the ship sailed on, its luminous effervescent wake trailing behind it. It bore away to pick up speed. M'Baraï thought that the schooner was skimming along so it could then veer around and come back to pick him up but the slave ship kept sailing on. Slowly, her tall, dark sails, unfurled like the wings of Satan, became smaller and smaller, eventually disappearing into the black of the night.

Alone in his whaleboat, without even a scrap of sailcloth, M'Baraï couldn't carry out any useful manoeuvre. He let himself drift in the trough of the sea and in the wind, all the while thinking less than comforting thoughts… The painter hadn't broken, no, as when he took it out of the water he'd pulled it along its whole length… it had either slipped out of the sailors' hands or, to borrow an English term, those *sons of bitches*[59] had let go on purpose to play a dirty trick on him, on M'Baraï, the bosun! But they couldn't leave him drifting like this… Once he was back on board he'd punish them good. Even if the Kanaks said nothing, the captain or the first mate would soon realise he was missing and the schooner would turn around and come back to pick him up… if only to get the whaleboat which was worth money. And then the sailors would be in for it – never would they ever do anything like that to him again!

The breeze came up again and the light craft drifted like a bit of cork, abandoned and at the mercy of the wind and the waves. Towards the west, at a distance impossible to judge in the night, M'Baraï saw a line of mountains, which he thought was Malekula Island.

Still looking in the darkness to where the schooner had disappeared to see if it was coming back for him, M'Baraï's thoughts turned to the little popinée of Aoba, his popinée, who was still on board, and he felt miserable. Then, by a process of linking ideas related to a number of different incidents, he concluded that the Kanaks had dropped the whaleboat's painter on purpose to do away with him so they could use and abuse his woman. And one of those who had dropped the painter, a Kanak from Ouvea, regarded as the best sailor, would succeed him in the shipboard hierarchy – and he was also one of those who had sought out his popinée and found only M'Baraï's fists.

Having been used to the sea and all its dangers since his childhood, M'Baraï didn't think for one moment about his somewhat critical situation. Instead, he was tortured by pangs of jealousy. The whaleboat kept on drifting and the schooner wasn't coming back. He

---

59   Baudoux writes, "sons of a bitch" in English in his text.

mustn't spend his forces. He had to stay there, inert, waiting, waiting… While he waited, he gnawed at his fists, those enormous fists he wished he could use.

The south easterly started to weaken and, little by little, it stopped. The waves made lapping sounds as they broke on their crests before quietly flattening out. And all was calm… Only the great swells of the ocean continued to rock him gently in their long, slow undulations.

The first pale light of dawn came over the horizon and lit up the sky. Soon the immobile whaleboat and its impatient-faced passenger saw the sun come up. But there was nothing, nothing at all… The sea was as still as glass and there was not a sail in sight. In the distance, mountains on the islands were visible through the mist.

III

It was dead calm the whole morning with not a ripple on the sea. Only a few schools of fish swimming about here and there tarnished the immense mirror. The reflection of the sun on the water intensified the heat in the air. Open to the elements, the whaleboat was scorching hot inside.

As Jean M'Baraï was born in this tropical climate he didn't suffer too much from the heat despite there being no shade at all. To cool his body and dampen his thirst, he immersed himself in the water a number of times. His only real pain came from him not having his pipe and tobacco. As for hunger, he didn't even think about it.

The sun was high in the sky, there was not a sail on the horizon and the wind had still not come up. M'Baraï began to weigh up his chances. He could get closer to one of the islands, whose mountains he saw in the distance, either by single oar sculling or rowing there standing up in his boat. But these islands were inhospitable, especially for a lone unarmed man. If he landed, he would be killed, roasted and eaten – so it really wasn't in his interests to go ashore. Another thing, he should stay where he was, in full sight, in the area where he had been abandoned, not close to the shore where the whaleboat would be less visible. On board the schooner he was certain they'd have put a lookout on the masthead to search for him and, more importantly, the whaleboat.

M'Baraï concluded that he should wait there, patiently, for the breeze… as the schooner had surely found herself becalmed and was thus incapable of moving. Then, as was the custom of island sailors, he started to whistle long and hard to make the wind blow. But Aeolus ignored his efforts.

At last, a change in fortune! As nightfall approached, clouds gathered in the distance to the east, and they came towards him in caravans propelled by the wind. The dark line of trembling water spread out over the sea. The breeze was coming. Very soon, it was caressing the whaleboat and its passenger with its coolness. Slowly, the wind became stronger and the boat began to drift gently. There was nothing yet in view but now that the breeze was up, the schooner would soon show herself towards Ambrym.

Time passed, the sun went down, the schooner still didn't come and the wind blew stronger.

Finally, M'Baraï began to worry. Were they going to abandon him? What was he going to do, alone, in this boat, without sails and without supplies? Where to from here?

Before nightfall, he saw a shiny speck lit up by the last rays of the setting sun on the horizon. This speck shone from a height, it was sails. M'Baraï, who had the eyes of both a primitive man and a purebred sailor, recognised his schooner. Darkness gradually descended and the sky clouded over.

It would be at least two hours before the schooner reached him. How would they find him in the dark? He didn't have any sort of light to alert them to his presence. It would be up to chance alone. The wind blowing in from the east pushed him closer to Malekula Island.

Lying in the trough of the sea, the whaleboat took on sea spray and was drifting too quickly. M'Baraï resolved firmly to stay where he was, to wait for the schooner and not to let himself be carried off to Malekula, which was coming alarmingly closer by the minute.

He took the oar at the back of the boat and began to scull with all his might. All he could do was keep the boat upright against the waves, in its position, without any possibility of moving forward. For more than an hour and with typical M'Baraï doggedness, he managed to keep the boat in place. But, in the end, as the wind became increasingly more violent, he was beaten by a blast of wind and a giant wave that ejected the little boat and set it adrift like a dead leaf.

Faced with the ineffectiveness of his efforts and the danger he would be in if he let the boat fill up with water, M'Baraï had no choice but to flee with the wind at his back, ahead of the squall that was pushing him towards Malekula Island. Land was fast approaching.

The wind howled in the night, the rain lashed against the boat and the light craft bounced in the troughs of the waves. Sometimes it slid like a toboggan on the salty, white, foamy breakers.

The coast stretched out before him, black and mysterious. In the darkness he couldn't make anything out. The landing was swift – a savage swell that didn't want to break on its own, lifted up the whaleboat and smashed it against the rocks. M'Baraï extricated himself from the sea by acting as if he were an invertebrate so as not to break his back. Feeling his way, he climbed the craggy rocks that left his hands and feet bloodied. He found a crevice where he took shelter from the driving wind and rain. Then M'Baraï fell into a state of apathy – he lost both physical and mental feeling and this made him accept the situation he found himself in.

Not long after the storm, which only lasted a short while, the night became clearer, the sea calmed down, the sky was lit up by all its stars and Jean M'Baraï saw, not more than a mile away, the lights of his ship, and her black silhouette, sailing back the way she had come towards the south. Was the schooner still looking for him or was she leaving for good?

And then Mother Nature, imposing her laws upon this man in distress, put him into a deep sleep.

IV

When Jean M'Baraï woke up the sun was already beaming down on him. There was not a sail on the water as far as the eye could see … After the storm that night, the captain must have thought he was a goner and decided that it was pointless to keep up the search. Hunger gnawed at his stomach and his throat was completely dry from thirst. Despite his pressing need to find some sort of sustenance, he had to act cautiously if he didn't want to become cannibal fodder himself.

M'Baraï came out of his hole making himself as small as he could and climbed higher up the scrub-covered rocks. He examined the area, looking all around him: close to the coast to the northwest, far from where he was, were several little smoking islands. Along the coast, clumps of coconut palms extended their light foliage all silvery and shimmering. And there were forests as far as the eye could see – forests lining the valleys and covering the mountains up to their peaks.

He decided to head for the coconut palms, those providential trees that would give him both food and drink. To get there, he had to hide, walking through the undergrowth and not moving too far from the sea. After having listened to all the noises around him and having found an explanation for all of them, he shot a final glance around to make sure that there were no islanders in his vicinity. Then he went into the forest, which soon became almost impenetrable as trees of different heights and widths were so close to each other and were intertwined by adventitious roots and networks of lianas.

In this dark, damp, hot forest with its waterlogged floor, soft with humus and dead leaves piled on top of each other, in this mysterious forest, full of unknown things about which he had no concept, M'Baraï, the man of the sea, was a fish out of water. His simplistic mind had retained something of the ancestral superstitions of the New Caledonian Kanaks. The slightest noise raised his suspicions – branches swaying in the wind, crackling as they rubbed against each other, seeds coming loose and falling heavily to the ground, birds who flew off beating their wings or screeching like savage warriors, the tree trunk in the shape of a deformed man, patiently waiting and watching, and the other tree behind which a devil was surely hiding. Everything seemed to him to be the threats of invisible beings who wanted to kill him. The danger that he could sense, but remained unknown, frightened him – he would have preferred to see it, to throw himself at it furiously, to end it. To give himself courage, he pulled his sailor's knife from its sheath and assured himself that its long blade was very sharp. Then he continued to slither like a reptile through the inextricable vegetation of the tropics.

He had been moving for a good while when he heard, attenuated by the distance, the sweet and monotonic sound of running water. As fast as possible, he headed towards this deliverance from the thirst that was tormenting him, without even stopping to pick some leaves of the edible cabbage trees he passed on the way. He had to do first things first.

After what seemed to him a very long time, he came to the edge of a stream that passed through a little clearing. There he was pleased to see a few coconut palms whose slender trunks were weighed down by their long leaves drooping in the stifling humidity, some wild banana trees growing in thick clumps and some breadfruit trees – a feast lay before him.

These fortunate finds, the fantastic clarity of day and the blue sky lifted his spirits. Everything looked as if it would turn out all right. M'Baraï was no longer thinking about black cannibals, his only concern was to eat and drink his fill. When he had appeased his hunger and thirst, he was overcome by lethargy. He lay down on the grass and began to contemplate his new situation on the island.

So he could keep an eye out for the slave ships that would certainly come and drop anchor near the coast, and he could then take his chance to get on board by whatever means necessary, he shouldn't go too far inland. What's more, the sea would supply him with fish and shellfish. The trees would continue to provide him with fruit. His material life was thus assured – he didn't have anything to worry about there. But he still had to hide and not leave behind any clues that would reveal his presence to the natives. Above all, he mustn't light a fire, something that would have been easy for him to do the Kanak way, by rubbing two sticks together.

He then remembered when, on his first trip on the schooner, they had dropped anchor in a bay in the south of the island where two Anglican pastors and a number of Samoan natives had settled. Later, his ship had recruited Kanakas on the west coast, bartering with the chiefs: two long-headed niggers for a Schneider shotgun and a hundred cartridges.

He decided very quickly on his plan. He had to go back to the pastors in the south, on the windward side of the island. To do so, he would have to keep himself hidden, passing through the forest by day and following the coast by night.

In readiness for a possible attack, and in order to defend himself, he cut a heavy root hanging in the water and shaped it into a club. Jean M'Baraï then set about making a shelter. He walked a few steps into the dark forest and caught sight of a huge banyan tree, which he climbed. There, in a bundle of leafy lianas, he fashioned himself a sort of natural hammock. After testing it, he felt quite satisfied with his work.

To guard against any eventuality, he hung his club within reach and stuck his knife in the sheath he had taken from his belt. He then curled up in a ball, invisible in his verdant nest.

And so night came. It stretched slowly across the landscape, erasing the contours of the trees which disappeared into the intense obscurity of the forest. Nocturnal insects fluttered, crackling their elytra. Flying foxes left their refuges, flying sluggishly, their viscous wings brushing the tops of the leaves. They then hung from the branches, looking for wild figs, and soon the piercing screeches of their rutting battles shattered the calm of the night.

Still haunted by his superstitions, M'Baraï was not sleeping. He was there alone, without any moral support, at night, in the middle of this unfamiliar forest, in the shadows which for him concealed countless terrors. There had to be devils there too, just as there were in New Caledonia, and devils could see clearly at night – they have red eyes and can climb trees and people cannot kill them.

To comfort himself, he watched the stars through the branches, twinkling, as if on purpose, to send him signs. The bats and the insects didn't bother him – he knew them. But the strange sounds coming from the undergrowth, sounds that were amplified by the silence, made him somewhat uneasy.

He heard a muffled din, far away, coming from the dark, shadowy depths of the forest. Then, many hurried footsteps and laboured, angry breathing. No doubt about it – it was either ferocious Kanaks or the devils from this island. If he didn't move, these furious beings would perhaps pass by without seeing him. This thought was only partly reassuring… he took his knife in one hand and his club in the other. The infernal horde was coming closer… it was there! He heard shrieks, moans, groans… and he finally realised that it was a pack of wild pigs sniffing, grunting and jostling each other with their snouts as they searched for food on the forest floor.

As the pigs were there, it meant that there was neither human nor devil in the vicinity, as these pigs, who had become very wary in their wild state, would have run off straight away.

Reassured on this account, M'Baraï relied on the pigs to watch his back. He then slipped off into the ethereal depths of oblivion and dream.

V

The next morning M'Baraï woke up, refreshed in body and mind. After having eaten and gathered a stock of breadfruit and coconuts, his club in hand and his knife in his belt, he set off across the forest towards the south. He kept his head down the whole time.

He kept the morning sun to his left as a guide - whenever it was possible to glimpse it through a hole in the forest canopy. He avoided moving away from the coast as much as he could. So he could get an idea of the distance between himself and the coast, from time to time he climbed trees, but he only saw the sea on the distant horizon without being able to judge where the coastline was. M'Baraï was following the plateau of a mountain range the base of which he couldn't see. In spite of that, he kept going forward.

When the sun was at its highest, M'Baraï, sweaty, breathless and tired of freeing himself from the lianas, hadn't made much progress. He stopped for a rest.

Sticking with his idea to head south, but walking a bit less enthusiastically, he set off again in this direction. He hadn't gone far when he came across a fairly clear track. Was it a track made by the frequent passage of wild pigs or Kanaks?

Tracks created by wild boars are narrow and deep in the ground, low lying branches at the height of the animals are never broken but are always soiled by the muddy backs of the creatures who rub against them as they go by.

Kanak tracks are also made by feet that always tread the same path. There are no traces of marks made by picks or axes and they are wider and shallower than pig tracks. But here, as he had sidestepped the obstacles, only the little branches at human height had been bent or broken. As for footprints, these could easily be confused as Kanaks and wild pigs used each others' tracks.

Having examined it, M'Baraï recognised that this track was mostly frequented by people. He thought it prudent to move away from it and continued on his way through the forest.

He had scarcely started moving again when he heard the rustling of bushes. He turned his head and saw fifteen or so Kanaks, naked and very black, following each other silently in single file along the track like shadows in the forest. Two of them were armed with rifles, the others had bows and arrows. In the presence of this visible, known danger, M'Baraï was hardly shaken. He concealed himself behind a tree trunk. The Kanaks went past without making a sound, disappearing into the thickness of the vegetation.

M'Baraï realised that he was in an inhabited area and that he should first study his surroundings and double his precautions before going any further.

He didn't go more than a few steps at a time whenever he moved, taking care not to make any dead branches or dry leaves crack underfoot. Before shifting, he listened and looked all around him to make sure there was nobody there. Finally, he stopped and clambered up a very tall tree with dense foliage.

When he was on the highest branches, M'Baraï saw in front of him, but a stone's throw away, a few straw huts perched on the mound of a hill in a narrow clearing. Then, a bit further, in a dip leading down to the sea, some wisps of smoke rose towards the forest. It was a Kanak village. His route to the south was blocked.

It was already late. M'Baraï stayed in his tree, settling in the best he could to spend the night there. At the same time he wanted to observe the comings and goings of the Kanaks and figure out his plan of action for the next day.

When night fell, the cacophonous racket of a great gathering of people rang out from the depths of the forest. Then the sound of dull pounding on hollow trees could be heard. These "booms" came from tree drums, hollowed out like canoes and standing upright, whose muffled sound waves carried over several miles. Other giant xylophones, similar to the drums but standing at great distances from them, answered, making a chorus. The mountains and forests echoed these noises, which grew in number and in strength, and soon it was a hellish din like the rumble of a cataclysm.

Mixed in with this powerful bass made by the resonating trees, were wild screams, the howls of ferocious beasts and the bellowing of furious bulls, all of which rose and fell in turn. Then it was the heavy, subterranean thuds, beat out by thousands of feet hitting the ground together, under the weight of a jumping human mass.

M'Baraï knew what it was, having heard it already at night on board his schooner when it was moored. It was the cannibal islanders doing their 'sing-sing', a big feast where they ate pork and human flesh while dancing the pilou.

These infernal celebrations, which had probably come from the anthropoids, continued, loud and relentless. Natives brandishing torches moved about in all directions, lighting the forest below. When they appeared naked, black and glistening with sweat, hideous in their halo of hectic light, they looked like gorillas or the devils of Kanak legend. But seeing them like this, M'Baraï did not fear them as, afterall, they were but black men and they would never find him in his tree.

The forest, or rather the valley that, he guessed, lay before him, was inhabited by an important tribe that blocked his way, but no matter! Tomorrow, he would take another route south - he'd either go a bit higher on the mountains or lower along the seashore – at night under cover of darkness.

Just before daybreak the drumming and the ruckus ceased and the natural environment returned to calm. Only the forest branches still rustled in the gentle breeze.

M'Baraï had his plan all worked out. As soon as he was able to see where he was going, he came down from his tree and made his way to the sea, moving as quickly as possible through the forest. In a few clearings, under the coconut palms, he saw some huts as he went by but he didn't worry about it. He wanted to go fast. His club in hand, his stocky body supple, he walked on, conscious of his strength, determined and formidable.

In next to no time he was on the shore. He stopped to take a look around. A beach lined with coconut trees stretched out in front of him. It was low tide and a few beached dugout canoes were sitting up on the sand about 200 paces to the south.

M'Baraï stripped naked. He made a little packet of his clothes, wrapped it in leaves and tied it up with lianas. Then he hurried off in the direction of the dugouts, keeping to the water's edge. He went past the huts under the coconut palms without slowing down. When he got to the dugout canoes, he looked inside, took a spear and kept going. A bit further on, some more huts came into view. In front of them, he saw a rack of woven lianas held up by some short stakes – it contained yams and cooked fish. He took a few strides over to take his share. Then he left, quickening his pace and keeping to the water's edge all the way so he could swiftly reach the rocks of a foothill that jutted into the sea.

When he got to the rocks he climbed them before getting dressed and throwing his spear, which had become useless and cumbersome, into the sea. He entered the forest, heading towards high ground. When he thought he had gone far enough, he stopped, sat down on some roots and started eating the spoils of his little act of larceny.

While he ate, he smiled, as he was satisfied with himself. Now the mysterious sounds of the forests no longer scared him – he was used to them. And he had really screwed those Kanaks over. He knew that after a night of pilou and big kai-kai,[60] the Kanaks were tired and would all sleep soundly until the sun was at its peak. He had undressed so as not to be recognised. If the Kanaks had seen him from afar, they would have taken him as one of their own with light skin. He had walked on the sand at low tide because his footprints would be washed away when the tide rose. And his footprints were just like those of other men – the Kanaks would find nothing out of the ordinary.

When he had eaten his fill, he charged back into the bush, still heading south.

His enthusiasm for pushing on through the dense bush and curling lianas was soon dampened. His legs felt weak, dizziness overcame him, he had to stop. He tried several times to get going again but each time he only managed a few steps before he had to sit down. Finally, like a wounded animal, he lay down on the ground, drained of all his strength.

Then he started trembling and shaking, a cold sweat broke out on his forehead and invaded his body. His teeth began chattering and he felt as if he had plunged into an icy bath. He

---

60   Feasting.

regretted not having a blanket or fire to warm him up. If he could have lit a fire, he wouldn't have hesitated for an instant as he was no longer afraid of the Kanaks. All that mattered to him was getting warm. Indeed, warmth meant everything to him.

The only serious thought that crossed his mind was a really miserable one – the yam and the fish he had taken from the Kanaks, and then eaten too greedily, were poisoned, he just knew it. And now he was going to die there, alone, in this forest and no one was going to come to his rescue. When he died, the crows, rats and wild pigs would come and devour his corpse and that would be the end. All that would remain would be his bones scattered on the ground.

He got used to this idea. Faced with the inevitable, he accepted it. He shivered with cold and fever and, almost unconscious, he waited to die. Then a warm feeling came over him, almost one of well-being, but it didn't last. His body was burning and his throat was parched by a blazing thirst. He got up to fetch some water and his head spun, he was dizzy. Unable to take more than a few steps and feeling unable to go on, he lay back down. Then came the sweats that alternated between hot and cold. Finally, he felt as if he had disappeared and fallen into a black hole.

M'Baraï woke up in the middle of the night with a clear mind. He was no longer ill but very tired and his muscles ached all over. "So the Kanaks hadn't poisoned him afterall...", he thought to himself remembering the night's events. Now he knew what sickness had befallen him – all the whites who stayed on the islands got it. He'd seen Europeans with this illness come aboard the ship looking either for medicine or to leave this country where they could no longer bear to live. He'd caught the malarial fever of the New Hebrides.

As soon as daylight broke, M'Baraï set off, still planning on seeking refuge with the Anglican missionaries. His legs had a hard job carrying him and his strength soon left him. The short distance he travelled was done painfully. Despite it all, he was making some headway.

In the afternoon, he was unlucky enough to stumble into an inhabited area. He was forced to stop, as a precaution, and to study what lay ahead, before pressing on. Then a bout of fever, like the one he had had the day before, overcame him. He suffered all the torments and shivered as he huddled up between the roots of a banyan tree.

The next day, he spent what little energy he had hiding from the Kanaks that he had seen and finding himself some food. He knocked down coconuts and ventured into a plantation to gather bananas that he found in abundance. Towards nightfall, he had his bout of fever, which succeeded in making him waste his day. He hadn't found a favourable place to cross the region that was inhabited by the natives. He had walked, crawled and turned around in circles. He pulled out bunches of grass to sleep on and wedged himself in between some boulders in the forest.

During the night, M'Baraï felt weak but didn't have it in him to try to get down to the sea to go around the coast under the cover of darkness. Struck down with malaria, his energy had abandoned him.

The next day, without leaving the forest, he headed painfully towards the mountains, to pass over the top of the Kanak tribes if he could. But even up there he found forest clearings where he saw clusters of huts and lots of natives of both sexes. On several occasions he nearly showed himself – he had just enough time to hide before beating a hasty retreat. In spite of this, spurred on by hunger, he went back and managed to enter a plantation where he silently cut some sugar cane. Then he went back into the depths of the forest to find refuge. He crammed the driest leaves he could find into the length of the trunk of a fallen tree. Victim of another bout of fever, he stretched out, discouraged, on his bed of crackling leaves.

In the night, large drops of water pattered down upon the forest canopy. The sound grew louder and louder, becoming relentless.

The tropical downpour, brought in by the squall, had soon penetrated the thick canopy. Spears of rain shot through it, streamed down the branches and the bark on the tree trunks, splattered on the saturated ground and seeped in everywhere.

And poor M'Baraï, still shaking with fever, crouching at the foot of a tree, with his sodden clothes stuck to him, received this deadly downpour, full of resignation before the irremediable.

The rain kept pelting down, heavy and penetrating, for hours and hours. Ponds filled, channels formed, streams broke through their obstructed courses, silt-laden waters flowed in torrents down the precipices and ravines and rolled in avalanches to the bottom of the valleys, uprooting any trees in their way.

When day came, it was no longer raining – but rain still came down from the multitude of forest leaves. M'Baraï got undressed, wrung out his clothes to get rid of the water, before tying them up with a liana. Next, he chewed on some sugar cane. Once his breakfast was finished, he tightened his belt. He checked that his knife was firmly in its sheath, slung his bundle of clothes over his shoulder, picked up his heavy club and, naked in the undergrowth, set off, still bent on going to higher ground.

He wanted to find a passage in the forest, above the region that was inhabited by the natives, and then resume his journey southward. In his head, he couldn't have been very far from the clergymen's camp. By way of the various sounds he heard, he knew that Kanaks were still in the proximity – so he took even more precautions.

With the clouds dispersed, the sun appeared through the foliage. M'Baraï rejoiced. He continued weaving his way through the bush more fervently than before, not feeling his weariness. He imagined that the night's rain had done him good.

In a spot in the forest, M'Baraï saw a big ray of sunlight cutting through the branches forming a square of light on the ground, making the floating specks moving through the air sparkle. He made his way over to the square of light. When he was there, he hung his clothes from low-hanging branches to dry them. Then, he sat down on a root and, quite exposed, basked in the sun to warm himself up.

As the gentle heat penetrated his skin, the half-caste became drowsy like a lizard. His lazy thoughts wandered idly… He saw New Caledonia again, his father and mother, the schooner and the popinée from Aoba. Completely relaxed, time passed without M'Baraï realising it.

Then, he leapt to his feet with a start and pricked up his ears – he had heard the crackle of leaves and dry sticks. He looked all about. Nothing. A few almost imperceptible noises came to him. M'Baraï lay down on the ground to listen and see further into the forest. After a bit, he made out, camouflaged in the dark mêlée of the underbrush, some fantastical beings, black and ape-like, who moved, stopped and hid to advance upon him. M'Baraï wanted to retreat and take up a defensive position against the trunk of a huge tree. Piercing shrieks rang out from all sides. He was surrounded. In an instant, he was encircled by a horde of savages who threatened him with their weapons all the while howling furiously.

At that point Jean M'Baraï's half-caste blood revealed itself with all its force – he had both the stubbornness and the courage of a Breton teamed with the cat-like agility and ferocity of a New Caledonian Kanak warrior. Brandishing his heavy club in his right hand, his knife held firmly in his left, he lunged forward and rushed into the diabolical circle which, stopped by the tangled mess of the forest, couldn't widen enough in time. M'Baraï smashed heads, opened bellies and jumped on bodies. When a spear met its mark, he pulled it out with a reverse stroke of his club so as not to be hindered. Faced with the nimbleness and rapid-fire blows of the half-caste, the circle of assailants widened but didn't break. Losing blood, M'Baraï kept on charging and causing fatalities. Not wanting to injure each other, the Kanaks, who were wound up in the trees and lianas, couldn't hit this elusive, frightening man with their numerous arrows. One arrow ended up embedding itself in M'Baraï's shoulder but he kept up his attack. Then he fell face forward on the ground. A Schneider bullet had passed through his chest.

The Kanaks let out great cries and yells of triumph.

VI

The seas of green, which were the forests covering the mountains, glistened in the dazzling sunlight. The light breeze dancing through the leaves made long shimmering waves and the sleepy flora rustled. In the hazy distance, under a white line of immobile clouds, the sky mingled with the Pacific Ocean.

On a dome that rose up straight from the dark forests stood a few slender coconut palms, their long fronds gently swaying. Low huts, lying quite flat to the ground, were nestled under the shade of the palms. Clumps of bamboo, which were dotted haphazardly around this indigenous camp, rustled and rattled in the slightest breeze.

In one of these huts, Jean M'Baraï opened his eyes and slowly regained consciousness. The very low roof seemed like it was coming down to smother him… He was lying on a mat on the ground… Some old Kanaks were sitting around him… A small fire warmed his feet… Why was he there?

A white-haired Kanak with a hard face noticed that the half-caste had woken up. He came closer to him, shuffling on his bottom. Then he cracked open a coconut and poured the milk into M'Baraï's mouth. M'Baraï took a big mouthful. As soon as he swallowed, he felt a sharp pain, like someone had driven a stiletto into his chest. He stopped drinking. But he was thirsty, the coconut was there over his mouth, and he drank again, slowly this time and it wasn't as painful. Then the old Kanak took away the coconut.

What was this evil thing that made him suffer so badly? Why had he, M'Baraï, come here? He didn't even know these old Kanaks, did he?

Little by little it came back to him… Black creatures jumping around him trying to kill him. Devils. The dull blows of his club on their skulls and the small of their backs. His long knife plunging into their flesh. Warm blood splattering over him. The spear in his thigh. The bodies he slid over. The Kanaks who retreated before him, leaping backwards into the lianas. So he hadn't killed them all then? And his memories became confused. In a fainting fit, his eyes closed and he fell into a coma again.

In the night M'Baraï woke up. The flickering flames of a small fire lit up the inside of the hut that was blackened by smoke. Two Kanaks were sitting next to him with their weapons at their sides. They were watching over him. The sound of rhythmic breathing told him that other Kanaks were sleeping around the hut.

The half-caste feigned sleep so as not to attract the attention of his guards. Then he tried to gather his thoughts to understand why he was there. The events whizzed through his mind – the schooner, the shipwreck, the forests, the battle. He knew he was lying there, wounded, as a spear had pierced his thigh. To make sure, he contracted his leg muscles and the pain told him he was right.

But why did the right side of his chest hurt too? It was painful when he breathed. Maybe he'd received a bad blow? How did he come to be in this hut? He knew he hadn't got there alone. So the Kanaks must have brought him there. But why? ... As he searched for an answer to this bothersome question, a question that soon became of little interest to his weakened state of mind, he fell asleep.

When day came, the hideous old Kanaks, witchdoctors and takatas,[61] crouched around the now conscious half-caste and gave him all the care that their practical science afforded them. Four hands held him in a sitting position with his back straight. Three sticky mouths laboriously chewed a mixture of tree bark. Then they blew the saliva and plant fragments into his wounds where they stuck fast.

To the right of his battered bronze thorax, M'Baraï saw a gaping hole, red with coagulated blood. Under the insufflations of the chewed material, the red was turning green. It seemed to him that this hole had been made by a spear or a bullet. He also had a wound on his back as a Kanak was spitting underneath his right shoulder blade as well Another takata worked on his left shoulder – it must have been injured too.

Next, the old doctors of primitive medicine softened in the heat of the fire and by rolling them in their hands wide, thick and greasy leaves that they applied like compresses on the wounds. On top of these they put boiled banana leaves and then some pieces of a type of felt made out of tree bark. They then rolled everything up and tied it with woven fibres.

And the "Faculty of Medicine" moved on to the left thigh. The patient was laid carefully on his back, his leg was elevated, held vertically to make the operation easier, and things proceeded as they had for his chest. These bandages were replaced every two days.

A variety of foods in large quantities were placed within M'Baraï's reach. The full range of Kanak cuisine was represented. M'Baraï decided to eat some yam and fish and drink some coconut milk.

When he had been made comfortable, all the while suffering from his injuries, M'Baraï considered his present state. These cannibal Kanaks hadn't killed him, though they well could have. And now they were nursing him back to health. They tried as much as they could not to hurt him. They even brought him food. Why? ... A horrible though entered his mind – these savages wanted to get him better and fatten him up to kill him and eat him

---

61   A "takata" (from English "doctor") is a Kanak doctor or healer.

like, as the English said, a pig. They had no other objective. This thought haunted M'Baraï.

Armed guards watched the half-caste, day and night. Unable to understand their language, he couldn't catch anything of their rare and mysterious exchanges. He tried a few times to speak to them in bichelamar but they did not answer him.

Days passed sadly by for M'Baraï, still haunted by the thought of being eaten. Despite frequent bouts of malarial fever, the strength of youth gained the upper hand in the body of this strong nineteen-year-old half-caste. His wounds healed and his energy returned, even though he ate only the strict minimum so as not to put on weight.

The more his health improved, the more men were put on guard duty. In spite of everything, he still held out a little hope. Sometimes they'd take him outside to be in the sun. He would look at the sea in the distance and the forests that stretched out below him. He studied the layout of the land and identified inhabited areas by the smoke rising from them. M'Baraï planned his escape – when he was strong enough, he could knock down his guards, take them by surprise and grab their weapons, then escape into the forest and hide. Then he'd go to the sea, steal a canoe and leave on a tailwind and go wherever it took him – another island, a place where white people lived or, if he were lucky enough, he might come across a ship. If he didn't manage to escape, he would defend himself to the death - that is when the Kanaks had made up their minds to kill him. And, who knows, he might have the upper hand.

The savages were probably waiting for a special occasion to eat him – maybe a ceremonial feast, a sing-sing or a pilou.

VII

One night, M'Baraï was woken abruptly by a number of hands weighing down on him. In the blink of an eye he was bound hand and foot. He struggled and twisted, round and round like a worm, shouting with rage, powerless to do anything. But the hands held him down flat on the ground so that he wouldn't damage his body. Exhausted by his efforts, he slowly calmed down, understanding that the end was nigh. With apprehension mixed with impatience, he awaited the blow that would finish him off.

The next day, strong arms lifted the half-caste, took him out of the hut and lay him in a crude hammock made of lianas and padded with grass. The hammock was carried by three Kanaks at each end of a long pole. The caravan, made up of a hundred or so individuals, set off and entered the forest. Everyone was walking in Indian file, or rather, Kanak file.

The men in the front cut lianas, parted branches and prepared the way for the others. From time to time, without slowing their pace, those carrying M'Baraï were replaced. At one point they made a stop. An old takata that M'Baraï knew by sight poured some coconut milk into the half-caste's mouth and the caravan continued on.

Where were they taking him? To a tribe where there were many savages so they could kill him ceremoniously in their presence? It would have been better if they'd knocked him out while he slept. Now they were going to torture him, kill him slowly and take pleasure in his suffering before biting into his flesh. Sometimes M'Baraï had fits of rage – he screamed out insults and writhed about in his hammock making his carriers lurch out of their straight line.

Throughout these lugubrious reflections, the caravan kept on, marching forever forward – it climbed up, went down and climbed again, remaining in the forest until coming to a plateau where the vegetation was not as thick. Buried in the grass of his hammock, M'Baraï could only see what was above him. He saw trees, more trees, then the sun, some bamboo plants and coconut palms. The scenery changed. His hammock brushed the tops of rows of posts as it went past. He went through a door. The carriers went on for a few more steps and stopped. The hammock was put down on the ground. He was going to die there! As he was unable to defend himself, M'Baraï closed his eyes.

The savages released the half-caste from the lianas and the straw in the hammock. Then they undid the ropes that were tied around his legs and feet. M'Baraï opened his eyes, glanced fiercely at the savage beasts that surrounded him… So they weren't going to kill him straight away after all… Why weren't they finishing him off? He still had his arms tied to his body and couldn't hit them, these brutes who were going to torture him.

Two Kanaks took M'Baraï by the shoulders and helped him up. He did not see a single homicidal gleam in any of the sparkling eyes that were looking at him. One Kanak came up to him and spoke to him in bichelamar. He said, "House here belong you, you stop here all time, me fellow give you plenty caïcaï. Suppose you want run away, me fellow kill you finish, after me fellow caïcaï you."[62]

The Kanaks parted in front of M'Baraï so that he could see two huts a few steps away. The speaker continued. "You look house here belong you sleep. Other one belong women, five women stop here belong you married. You make good belong him, by and by you hear him he good. Now finish."

The Kanaks untied the hands of their prisoner and swiftly disappeared.

Free of his bonds and faced with the sudden change from morbid thoughts to the new life he was being offered, M'Baraï was dumbstruck. When he wanted to speak to the Kanaks, everyone had gone. He was alone.

His stunned air only lasted a short while. The half-caste soon regained his faculties and ended up finding that it all made sense. Since the Kanaks hadn't killed him straight away - they'd in fact nursed him back to health - they obviously didn't want to harm him. They'd trussed him up to carry him there so as to stop him from being violent on the way.

Happy with his lot, he then showed himself around. His place was surrounded and secured by a fence made of stakes higher than a man. At its widest point, his land measured 40 or so paces and a rivulet ran through it. A few trees and three coconut palms sheltered two new huts made of straw and reeds.

Bending down, he entered one of the huts. At the back, in the half-light, he made out some black human forms all crammed together, squatting. He went closer and the forms moved back, huddling together, heads went down, disappeared and all the arms and legs got mixed up, merging into one. And this live flesh became nothing more than a black homogenous mass. It was a group that the sculptor Carpeaux would never have imagined.[63]

M'Baraï tried to find a head or limb by feeling in front of him at random. He grabbed a warm and slippery arm and pulled. A popinée followed docilely, hiding her eyes with her free arm. He continued untangling the packet of flesh. In total he found five young, scared, fairly ordinary popinées. He later found out that they were very passive.

In the second hut that had been set aside for him, he saw a Kanak bed composed of a layer of straw with a mat spread out on top. The pillow was a log. A little fire was smouldering

---

62   Caïcaï = kai-kai meaning "food" and also "to eat".
63   Carpeaux was a renowned French artist in the period 1860-1875.

in the middle of the hut.

M'Baraï left his straw hut and once again surveyed his patch of land. He looked through a few cracks in the fence and saw that it was surrounded by huts and that there were sentries posted outside of the enclosure to keep guard.

Then he went back to see his harem. The ice had been broken. While the popinées were still ashamed and hid their faces, they did not huddle in the corner. They clumsily presented him with some local food.

With his women around him, M'Baraï had his first meal as a polygamist. Then, exhausted by the day's emotions and taken by a fit of malaria, he went and laid down on his mat, without worrying about what the next day would bring. Despite it all, things were working out well – life had some positives.

VIII

Jean M'Baraï the half-caste found himself immediately at ease in this sweet, indolent and hedonistic lifestyle. Having a strong penchant for sensuality due to his mixed Kanak and Breton blood, he developed a taste for the company of his women, so much so that soon this became his principal occupation, surpassing his other pursuits of eating and sleeping. His popinées were servile both by nature and through their meticulous Kanak education and so never caused him any problems or provoked any domestic quarrels due to jealousy or anything else. M'Baraï was the master at home – king of his enclosure.

Living alongside his women, he soon learned a few words of the not so complicated language of Malekula.[64] From time to time he received visitors – some notable Kanaks would take three stakes from the fence to open up a passage and then they'd take great pleasure in talking to him and asking the popinées whether they had all they needed and if they were in good health.

During these official, ceremonious visits, M'Baraï often saw the local man who, in bichelamar, had announced his deliverance and his new status as a Mormon. He learned that this Kanak was not just anyone. He had worked in Fiji for seven years for an English farmer who grew sugar cane and was involved in horse breeding. He'd been attached to the stud farm where he cleaned the stallions' stables and changed their bedding. Sometimes he'd take the mares out for a run to tire them before presenting them. Five other Kanaks from the tribe had also worked on this farm, which explained why they spoke a bit of English. It was rare that a day went by without M'Baraï receiving one of these visits.

M'Baraï was still seized frequently by bouts of malaria but little by little they decreased. He ended up getting used to them and not suffering from them as he had before. As he didn't exercise much and he ate a lot – meat, vegetables and fish – he grew strong. His neck became like a bull's once again and he even fattened up.

Fully satisfied physically, M'Baraï got bored and, without meaning to, began to make things complicated in his mind. Some days he longed for the sea – to see it, he climbed the highest coconut palm in the enclosure, made himself comfortable in the branches and

---

64   There are actually at least 30 languages spoken on Malekula.

stayed there looking at the big blue of the Pacific. Sometimes he'd see a sailing ship in the distance, sliding slowly through the immense sheet of water. He'd figure out the wind direction and the orientation of the sails and then, gradually, the ship would disappear on the horizon. And there M'Baraï would stay, imbued with a sadness that he couldn't define.

Still in his branches, thinking only of worldly things, he could see, far to the east, the thick, creeping smoke and the impressive glow that crowned the volcano on Ambrym Island. And below him, stretching as far as the sea, were the tops of the undulating forests. Then, there was the fence that surrounded him and around that, through the foliage, were the roofs of huts and his guards.

M'Baraï was always abundantly supplied with food – yams, sugar cane, meat and fish. He wanted for nothing. His popinées received the food already prepared, dished it up and served M'Baraï on leaves that stood in for plates. The lord and master ate everything that was put in front of him with gusto. He was fond of pork, especially when it had been well prepared, which happened sometimes – not often enough for M'Baraï though.

One fine morning when the playful sun was frolicking in the branches, M'Baraï, who was feeling happy with the world and was looking for something to do, decided to watch his sweet popinées unpack the food they had just received from the menfolk. From a basket made of woven coconut palm leaves, they took out yams and then some smoked fish, held stiff by little wooden skewers. Next they opened a smaller basket containing a package that had been carefully wrapped in banana leaves. The popinées undid it slowly, revealing pieces of bloody pig meat. The popinées quickly covered it back up with the banana leaves. Then, embarrassed, they pretended to busy themselves with the fish.

But M'Baraï, who had noticed this strange little manoeuvre, felt that the popinées wanted to deceive him. Why did they want to hide this kai-kai from him? Maybe they wanted to poison him?

M'Baraï brutally pushed the popinées aside and tore off the banana leaves. He saw dirty pink coloured skin with yellow stripes around a piece of meat. What was this unknown colour? … He looked more closely and suddenly recoiled in repugnance. Then he went closer again to see, to make sure he wasn't mistaken… he wasn't, it really was human flesh, there was no doubt about it. The black epidermis had been scraped off but on the thick dermis there were still the little spotted lines that the Kanaks made on their skin to make themselves more attractive. This flesh was a piece of a man's chest.

Suddenly, in a flash of perspicacity, M'Baraï realised that he had eaten human flesh! After having got rid of any trace of it being human, his popinées had served it up to him. Now he knew that this was the nicely prepared pork of which he was so fond. He spat with disgust, tried to make himself vomit but just couldn't do it. He looked for his popinées to beat them but they had disappeared.

M'Baraï, not easily shocked when he knew what he was dealing with, calmed down quickly and reasoned to himself, "Yes, he had eaten human flesh but he hadn't done it on purpose as he didn't know what it was. At the end of the day, he wasn't dead and he hadn't even been sick. But from now on, it was over, he wouldn't eat it again." He started pacing around his pen.

Seeing that their man was no longer angry, the popinées, who had been playing hide and seek with him, emerged, cautiously, their black faces expressive, exhibiting rows of very white teeth – cannibal teeth! M'Baraï understood that he couldn't make a scene as he was still at the mercy of these man-eating Kanaks. He too could be killed, have his skin singed and scraped off, and be cut up into pieces that would then be cooked and devoured. He felt repulsed by these black, naked women who ate human flesh. He watched them from a distance, no longer wanting to get close to them.

After a while, still keeping his distance, he spoke to them, explaining that it was very bad to eat human flesh, that white men did not do it and that this devil food would kill them.

Still smiling at him in the hope of getting back into his good books, the popinées responded by saying that human meat was better than pig meat, that they had to eat the Kanaks and popinées from other tribes when they were at war since the other tribes did the same and that the Kanaks of Malekula had always done this. The popinées did not want to accept that they could act in any other way. It was the custom to eat each other when they were at war, and they made war on purpose in order to do so.

Despite his stubbornness, M'Baraï, fearing he'd be put to death, did not try to convince the popinées. He felt that he could not singlehandedly reform the secular morals of Malekula Island. He left his women and sought refuge in his hut, intending never to have intimate relations with them again.

That night, when it was pitch black, when all was silent, the ancestral superstitions of the Ounouas came to torment the half-caste. He thought he heard noises, whispering devils and ghosts. He thought he saw some hiding in the dark corners of the hut. To reassure himself, he stoked his fire, adding wood to make it burn brightly and light up the places where the dead could come. He slept fitfully until morning.

The next day, M'Baraï thought again about the cooked human meat and his popinées who must have devoured the lot. He saw his women stretched out on the grass, warming themselves in the sun, completely undisturbed. They enjoyed their lives fully and were happy with the basic and instinctive sense of wellbeing they got from the sun in the sky. They seemed not even to remember the incident of the day before.

The unfortunate half-caste was appalled by the idea that his women ate human flesh. For a few days he bore a grudge against them. Then, little by little, he got used to the idea. He got close to them again and ended up finding the whole thing almost natural. After this cloud, life with his women returned to normal. Nonetheless, M'Baraï no longer wished to eat meat. When he saw a suspicious package, he would move away. Besides, his popinées took care to make any suspect pieces of meat disappear.

In this flimsy prison with fragile wooden walls, which was impossible to leave without immediately running the risk of being killed, the days rolled by, slowly and monotonously, one after the other. Filled up with food, sated by his women, even M'Baraï grew tired of this indolent lifestyle towards which he was naturally disposed. Now, he was truly bored and he would have liked to have had some space or been able to go for walks or gone to sea and fish. He had just added a fifth knot to a banyan leaf string, indicating that he had been locked up there for five moons. He made escape plans – the palisade would be easy to get over, under the cover of night he could reach the forest, hide and live there. But after, he would be tracked all over the island like a wild animal – he might fall into the hands of Kanaks more ferocious than those who currently held him prisoner.

M'Baraï chewed over his plans for several days, weighing up his chances to escape, when one morning he was surprised by the unexpected arrival of a number of Kanaks in his pen. What did they want? … Amongst them was the one who had worked for the farmer in Fiji, on the stud farm.

The Kanaks didn't seem hostile. They chatted amiably with the half-caste who, nevertheless, remained on his guard. Then they turned their attention to the popinées. So as to speak to them more closely, the Kanaks called two popinées, who they had already picked out in advance, by name. The two designated women approached, awkward and fearful, both preceded by an interesting rotundity. After discussing amongst themselves in learned assembly, the Kanaks conscientiously examined the bodies of the two women. Convinced by the undeniable evidence, they ordered the two impregated popinées to leave the *paddock*. This was done immediately.

They were taking his women away from him! M'Baraï wanted to shout out in protest, but he did not have time. Three replacements entered through the hole in the palisade – and he had come out on top – these ones were better, and there were three of them!

The Kanaks withdrew without giving the astonished half-caste any explanation of what had just happened – which seemed to interest them alone.

With this change of scenery, M'Baraï felt comforted and he abandoned his escape plans. What was the point of roaming the forests, risking being killed when he could stay there, care free, surrounded by his women? He forgot both the sea and the fish.

With the coming of the new moon, the half-caste added a knot to his string. They took another woman away from him and replaced her with a new one and so it continued. He ended up establishing a rollover that corresponded roughly to the number of knots in the string, a number that was forever on the up. Some popinées who remained slim were chastised by the Kanaks and replaced straight away.

As the knots in the string increased, the discipline became less rigid. One day, under the guard of a few armed warriors, M'Baraï was even invited to look around the village that encircled his prison. Two of them carried shotguns, the rest had bows and arrows.

These Malekulan Kanaks were less industrious than the New Caledonian Kanaks. Their forest huts, lit up by fire, were of the most rudimentary kind – a few coconut leaves or palm leaves over top of branches stuck in the ground, a bit of straw or reed and that was it. They had pigs that they kept in sties and seemed to value highly. M'Baraï saw popinées who, indifferent, attended to their business without manifesting any curiosity for his passage. He did not recognise any of his concubines amongst them.

After this, the Kanaks tolerated the half-caste walking around the outside of his paddock, so long as he didn't stray too far and he remained under the sleepy watch of his guards. Life continued on at this slow, sweet pace. He already had more than forty knots in his string.

M'Baraï thought and spoke only in Malekulan. It was only very rarely that he thought of the possibility of leaving. After having been quite put off by pork, he gradually rediscovered his taste for it, making sure, before eating, that he knew where the meat had come from. When he recognised human flesh, he simply left it, without making a fuss. His affable manner made him friends among the Kanaks and, as he never showed any intention of running away, he eventually became more of a prisoner on parole.

It had been a long while since his first popinées had been taken away from him and he didn't know what had become of them. Other concubines had spent their "season" in the pen, before being taken away, slim or fat. They had been replaced by new recruits, without M'Baraï ever seeing the same face twice. None of them came back. There was something mysterious about that, something he couldn't comprehend. As nobody wanted to explain why they changed his women, M'Baraï grew sick of uselessly scratching his head about it and he gave up. He simply lived.

IX

A great unrest prevailed in the Kanak village where M'Baraï was being detained. Some natives, members of the tribe, had had to beat a hasty retreat when faced with large numbers of attacking forces. After having seen their huts burnt and their plantations destroyed, they abandoned their pigs, their wounded and their dead. In a "run for your lives" situation, they had come to find refuge with their families, sowing seeds of panic in their wake.

The attackers, whose ranks were innumerable, were hereditary enemies from the North of the island. They were advancing in savage hordes, killing and destroying everything in their path, leaving only dead people, fires and ruins behind them. They revelled in orgies of human flesh. In brutish stupors, they raped children and corpses that they then devoured. It was the primitive race, the chosen ones, made in the image of god who followed their instincts, looking for the path to civilisation.

The number of fugitives kept increasing, swamping the village and creating a tremendous hullabaloo. The defence was organised and all the men armed themselves. There were stone axes, heavy clubs, spears hardened in the fire or tipped with human bone, and poisoned arrows. Then, there was a whole arsenal supplied over the years by passing traders: cheap trade rifles (more dangerous for those who used them), cast iron tomahawks, long bladed knives and steel harpoons.

The women, children and infirm old men took off, stealing silently through the bush, taking with them docile pigs and miscellaneous objects they held dear. The half-caste's harem joined this group of runaways.

From the gate of his pen, an excited M'Baraï watched the growing mass of assembling warriors who were now waiting with requisite calm for the battle to begin. The half-caste's fiery blood began to boil. He too would fight! He approached the warriors and spoke to the leaders he knew amongst them. He asked for weapons so he could fight alongside them.

The warriors consulted together. After a short wait, the Kanak who had been in Fiji went straight over to M'Baraï and handed him back his heavy club, the one he had used to such good effect in the past. He also gave him his knife in its sheath and his belt. Naked like the

Kanaks, M'Baraï, who had almost taken on the same hue as them, merged into the crowd.

Some lookouts who slithered along invisibly and silently like reptiles, came out of the thick forest and announced that the enemy was advancing in several groups. Still other sentries withdrew – the attacking forces were close.

The warriors who had been awaiting this signal, immediately scattered, disappearing behind trees and other natural refuges. M'Baraï followed their lead. In an instant, it was if the village had been abandoned.

The wind, like the forest's breath, was gently blowing through the leaves, making them rustle, and insects were humming. A few arrows whistled past and landed with a little ping in huts and tree trunks. The sly enemy was putting out feelers. The arrows continued to fly aggressively, their poisoned tips seeking out victims. Some of the warriors on M'Baraï's side could make out enemy figures in the shadowy undergrowth who were venturing out of their hiding places to raise their bows and take aim. They returned fire and in turn gave away their location. Thence commenced an exchange of arrows that left tree trunks looking like hedgehogs. Occasionally, a scream or a suppressed moan would escape – an arrow had met its mark. As the warriors grew more agitated, they showed themselves more and more. Shots rang out from both sides, the sound echoing in the mountains, seeming to go on forever.

In a frenzy brought on by the sight and smell of blood, the Kanaks neglected to stay under cover. To avoid the arrows, they doubled over, supple and cat-like, or jumped to the side. They even deflected them by batting them off with their weapons. They didn't think about the bullets. Bodies fell heavily, dead on the spot. Other victims rolled about on the ground screaming, trying to extricate themselves from the fight. Showing steely self-control, M'Baraï, having no throwing weapons, waited his turn, keeping hidden as best he could.

The relentless attacking forces kept advancing through the trees. The roars of these ferocious beasts made the forest tremble. The savage horde leaped forward like a dark wave breaking, smashing everything in its path and spitting forth a tide of black creatures, jumping, frenetic and brandishing all manner of lethal weapons above their heads.

M'Baraï, the first forward, absorbed the shock. His heavy, murderous club was put to work - he hit flesh and bone and saw individuals collapse around him. He opened up a pathway before him through the middle of the human wave. Encouraged by what they had seen, warriors from his side followed his example. It was a hellish, fast-paced mêlée above which rose cries of hatred and fury mixed with the lugubrious groans of the wounded.

Suddenly, more attackers rushed in from another side. The warriors in M'Baraï's camp were overwhelmed by the numbers and turned heel, beating a hasty retreat – soon it was a rout.

Tall flames crowned with thick smoke swirled up from the village. The attacking forces were victorious.

Sullied with blood, M'Baraï the half-caste and ten or so other Kanaks retreated step by step into the forest. They were followed by a group of stubborn opponents who didn't dare attack them, preferring to shoot arrows and bullets at them as soon as they showed themselves. The enemy Kanaks were afraid of this terrible man who was not of their colour and who was broader and stronger than other men. The heavy club and the red knife they could see in his hands drew their respect. Fearing an offensive from this diabolic man and his warriors, the Kanaks stopped pursuing them and went back to their own camp.

M'Baraï and his men withdrew to another village that belonged to the same nation. Night caught up with them in the forest but, as the Kanaks were in home territory, they were able to get their bearings. Before daybreak they were at a camp where many runaways had already gathered. More kept coming throughout the night. The next day, a few groups arrived pushing and dragging prisoners who looked like livestock destined for the abattoir.

In this speedy battle that had barely lasted five minutes, M'Baraï had been wounded twice – a bullet had ripped him open down the length of his ribcage and the other injury, which had been made by a blunt instrument, had split open his scalp, making a star shape but without smashing his hardy Breton-Kanak skull. The takatas treated his wounds, bringing all their skill and wisdom to bear.

X

Caught up in the joy of burning, destroying crops and feeding on human flesh, the victors stayed in the conquered village. They seemed not to want to go any further. They were too fearful to venture into a region that was almost completely unknown to them. They knew that the defeated Kanaks had had time to rally and welcome reinforcements from the entire tribe. Victory could no longer be assured. They did not advance further.

The vanquished tribe took all necessary precautions so they would not be taken by surprise. At the same time, they set numerous traps for their adversaries in case they decided to continue their victory march.

In the meantime, they needed to eat, quell their hatred and rejoice.

In the middle of a cold-blooded, ferocious crowd, beside the braziers being prepared to receive them, six nearly unconscious prisoners with crazed eyes and skin pale with terror were dragged along on their wobbly legs and held upright. Then, the victors proceeded according to the ritual. Hands with black claws held down a head, gripping it by the ears and the chin, wary of the drooling, foaming jaws that were snapping open and shut wanting to bite. A skilful butcher stepped forward holding a mace made out of a large black stone on the end of a handle. A dull blow to the back of the victim's head and his legs gave way. He collapsed, falling in a crouching position into the hands that were holding him. Blood streamed from his nose, mouth and ears. A final blow to his skull and the Kanaks laid his motionless body on the ground. A specialist wielding a long knife separated his head from his body. He located a joint between the vertebrates, under the neck, then he began cutting with his blade crunching along the jawbone as far as the chin. The severed head was left next to the corpse. And then it was on to the next one.

When in a last ditch attempt to save himself, a victim tried to put up a struggle, bellowing and rolling his eyes back in his head, the cannibal crowd would laugh, gleeful and gloating with pleasure. Finally, they came to the unlucky last!

Next, limbs were severed at the joints, bellies were opened and the victims were gutted. Pieces of flesh were carefully wrapped in thick leaves. Hot stones were put into chests then everything was placed in pits dug in the middle of the braziers of burning coals and incandescent stones. Water was poured over the packets of flesh, making a sizzling sound, but before it could all evaporate, the pits were covered over with earth, forming burial mounds until the meat was completely cooked.

The New Caledonian half-caste, who had lived for nearly four years with the Malekulan Kanaks, had adopted their mentality. He thought like them, took on their hereditary quarrels and loathed the tribe's enemies. It was not without a certain pleasure that he took part in the slaughter of the prisoners and all the ensuing operations. When it came time to share out the meat, he took his piece. But when he had to bite into the flesh, he didn't dare, he was overcome with nausea. So as not to compromise himself before his tribe, he pretended to eat before secretly getting rid of his horrible share.

The war was dying down, the invaders were no longer advancing. Things alternated between tracking, surprises, skirmishes and quick escapes. Sometimes there was feasting on human flesh.

With his injuries healed, M'Baraï became the most reputed warrior of the tribe and he took part, with a select group, in many of those aggressive sorties where cunning and strategy played a starring role. He taught courage and daring to these ferocious savages in whom these traits were lacking.

One night, after a successful raid, an old Kanak, in his admiration for the half-caste, let slip the following words: "When your sons grow up, we will be the strongest, we will beat all the other tribes, we will be the masters of Malekula."

But the old Kanak regretted having said so much, he checked himself and refused to say anymore. M'Baraï tried his best to get him to talk but the savage kept the secret of the elders and witchdoctors of the tribe sealed in his brutish head.

Leading the same life as the Kanaks, the half-caste knew how they poisoned the arrows that they used in warfare. They would poke them into the mush of decomposing pig snouts or they stuck them into the entrails of a putrefying corpse or else they would dip them into the sap of certain poisonous plants.

He also learned how to preserve the bodies of distinguished members of the tribe. When the cadaver had begun to deteriorate, when it was crawling with worms, the Kanaks would massage the decomposing flesh around the bones, mixing clay and fine straw into it. They coated the whole skeleton in this material, giving it back a shape that resembled that of a primitive man. They then smoked the cadaver until it dried, adding clay to the places that were disintegrating until the body became more or less solid. Next, the mummy was laid to rest in the local pantheon – either a cave, a hut or a banyan tree – for the great glory of the deceased and the tribe.

The war finally ended when the looters from the North found no more villages or crops to destroy or humans to eat. Lacking both food and the courage to push further south, they went back home.

The survivors of M'Baraï's former village and the Kanaks who had dispersed from the neighbouring area, joined together to form a new agglomeration in a valley close to the sea.

Huts went up quickly, then all the inhabitants, men and women, set to work planting yams and other crops. They also built pig pens in which to breed these animals that were symbols of wealth and luxury to the Kanaks of the archipelago.

M'Baraï remained free among the natives, with the same status as all the other individuals. He built his hut in the local fashion and tended his crops and pig pen. The Kanaks gave him two pigs and two popinées. This time they were real wives as tribal "specialists" broke two of their incisors to formalise their union.

Despite the availability of wild plant food sources, the sea became the main provider for the fledgling tribe while they awaited the harvest. The natives had a few dugout canoes and they hollowed out more tree trunks to expand their fleet. Fishing thus became *de rigueur*.

Jean M'Baraï saw salt water again! The sea… he touched it, immersed himself in it, and dove into it again and again to embrace it, take hold of it, possess it. To M'Baraï, the rocks beaten by waves and the beaches surrounded by shadowy forests seemed like the only wonders of the world. Instinct, not reason, drove him to admire everything to do with the sea – intricate lace coral, brightly coloured polypier trees, jellyfish that moved like dancing flowers and fish with polychromatic scales that seemed as if they were made out of metal or ceramic. Then, leaping up, his feet pointed so his toes broke the water's surface, M'Baraï would run silently with his arm raised, gripping his spear, to chase the fish. He speared them and they wriggled and quivered like quicksilver at the end of his weapon.

After his long sequestration spent in forest clearings, the first contact the half-caste had with the sea was unforgettably joyful. From this happy day, most of his time was spent on the beaches or in a dugout canoe, his spear in hand as his eyes scanned the clear waters. He sometimes caught a glimpse of sails, like a pair of white wings, appearing on the horizon. He would clamber onto the rocks to watch the sailing ship as long as he could – see it approaching, slowly, before turning and sailing away, leaving him only with the regret that the boat had not carried him off. A faint glimmer of his past burned in his heart before being quickly extinguished. M'Baraï, dispirited by this existence among the savages, fell back into the banality of his everyday life.

XI

M'Baraï's two popinées looked after the crops and the cooking. The half-caste took advantage of the easy, idle lifestyle of Kanak men and did not aspire to more. Sometimes his thoughts turned to his ex-lovers and his fatherhood. He made enquiries among some of the old Kanaks – his friends – but all that he learned was very vague. The Council of Chiefs and Elders expressly forbade him to see his ex-partners again. Similarly, they were never to see him again either. They were kept far away from him and he was not allowed to venture into their area or he would be killed on sight. Besides, the women had husbands. Yes, there were children that he had fathered but these children did not belong to him. That was all he had been able to find out.

In the end, M'Baraï did not worry about it any longer. He avoided wandering too far from the village so he wouldn't be killed if he accidently came close to his former wives. Life continued on in sweet indolence with his attention turned solely to fishing and the women who pleased him.

Since the formation of the new village, M'Baraï had noticed a young popinée who was barely nubile and whose shape, lighter skin tone, features and sparkling eyes made her more attractive to him than any other woman. No artifice was possible as the only clothing she wore was a liana around her waist and a tuft of grass in place of a fig leaf. Slowly, M'Baraï began to think about this young popinée... then he began to desire her. This became something of an obsession. He sought her out discretely but she would run away from him.

The half-caste heard through the grapevine that this young Melanesian beauty had been sold as a child to a powerful Kanak of a neighbouring tribe, who had paid her father in advance with ten fully-grown tusked boars. According to custom, a deal settled in this way was irrevocable and if it were broken, bloody conflicts would ensue. However, the owner did have the right to sell his property, if he wished, at whatever price he saw fit.

M'Baraï had thought of buying the young popinée but, according to the estimates made by those in the know, she was worth twenty tusked pigs at the very least. And he wasn't even sure whether her owner wanted to let her go. The poor half-caste, who had only two pigs that were still too young to have grown long tusks that curved around like bracelets, was not able to open up negotiations. He had to put a lid on his ambitions until wealth came into his pig pen.

Despite this setback, M'Baraï kept up his pursuit. He still paid attention to the beautiful brunette – but with great caution – as in these islands the jealous and the virtuous got rid of seducers and libertines by skilfully mixing poison into their food.

To get the girl to notice him, M'Baraï styled himself in the best Kanak fashion. He put flowers in his hair, tied a belt of lianas around his waist, decorated his wrists with boar-teeth bracelets and tied shells and fine cords around his ankles. He even used soot to blacken around his eyes. Not ugly like the Kanaks, the half-caste was already the best looking man in the tribe – now he was the most elegant too.

He would often meet the young popinée when he was fishing – he would speak to her and give her some fish. Sometimes he would see her with her companions in the plantations and he would give her wild fruit. The Black Venus, obeying the laws of nature that pushed normal beings towards the best, was not indifferent to the handsome half-caste's thoughtfulness and attention. Eventually, they both came to lust after each other. One day, the half-caste met the young popinée when she was alone. Her feminine mindset made her put up a struggle, while the beast offered himself to her and took her. She had purposely taken the same path as M'Baraï and did not complain about the incident to anyone.

And so things continued on like this. They met mysteriously, when rare occasions permitted it, far from the sleepy, yet sharp and observant, gaze of the Kanaks, who were like cats, always on the alert to see what was happening around them.

The liaison had been going on for scarcely a month when already the half-caste got the feeling - and then realised - that they were being watched. He had to be twice as careful and even secret rendezvous were no longer possible. One afternoon, M'Baraï was walking down a track when a poisoned arrow ricocheted off a tree next to him. He immediately hid behind the trunk - a second arrow came whistling towards him and was deflected by some lianas. This one had come from another direction. M'Baraï bent down to take cover and scoured the scene. He didn't see anyone. Remaining on watch and taking another path, he made his way back to his hut.

That day, he sharpened his knife on a stone and got himself a bow and arrows. From then on, he only ventured out on the tracks if he scanned any suspect bushes thoroughly. He only ate food that he had gathered and prepared himself. He came to be wary of his popinées and his friends as, intuitively, he knew that Kanaks were spiteful, shifty, cruel and cowardly. So as not to be taken by surprise when he was sleeping at night, he would go to bed in one place then, when all the village was silent, he would quietly move to another place to sleep. In spite of everything, some days he was able to make a few signs to his young accomplice who was also under the surveillance of the dark, initiated observers.

The half-caste understood that this shadowy, looming threat that worried him so much could not last for long. One day, he would fall victim to the patient, yet sure, vengeance of the Kanaks. If they hadn't already killed him in the open, it was because, having seen him at work, they were afraid of him. And there were a few Kanaks who would take his side and protect him. As, in similar cases that had happened within families or in the tribe, it was only the interested parties and their partisans who took charge of making whoever attracted their insidious condemnation disappear. Despite having fought for them, in their ranks, the natives still looked upon him as a foreigner and they never spoke of their business in front of him. If he came along, their conversations would stop. No Kanak told him that they wanted to kill him, but he could see it in their eyes that had become shifty.

M'Baraï was on his guard, distrustful and always ready to defend himself. He couldn't go elsewhere without the risk of happening upon another, almost certainly hostile, tribe. He also feared getting too close, without realising it, to the place where his ex-wives were living. This grave situation was further complicated by his attachment to the young popinée. This was no life! He would have preferred to see his avowed enemies before him and lash out indiscriminately, like a brute, and settle it once and for all. Waiting for an unseen and unknown danger that could arrive at any minute, sapped his untamed energy.

He spent nearly all his time on the seashore. He felt at home there and worried less about the danger. He could easily be taken by surprise and killed in wooded and bushy areas but on the beach or on rocks surrounded by water, he could see clearly.

One morning, as was his custom, the half-caste was on the rocks. He cast a glance towards the horizon and then towards the far-off mountains that were almost obscured by the mist. He saw a set of sails barely sketched out on the blue of the sea. He followed the sails with his eyes for a long time. Finally, he recognised a schooner that was approaching Malekula with wind on the quarter in its sails. M'Baraï started fishing, all the while taking an interest in the ship's progress.

The schooner kept coming closer, at one point it bore away then it passed, a few miles away, in front of the rocks where the half-caste was standing to get a better view. The ship continued on its route, making landfall.

An hour later, M'Baraï, who was anxiously following the schooner's progress, saw it enter a recess in the shore line then haul down its jibs, roll up its foresail and luff up. After a bit, the masts and cross-shaped spars glinting in the sun, stood out against the dark background of the wooded mountains. The ship had cast anchor near the coast - about five or six miles from where M'Baraï was, in the north-west.

Overjoyed, the half-caste went back to his shanty village. He told a few insignificant stories to the Kanaks. Then, remaining vigilant, he went around the communal women's huts as if he were looking for his women. He saw his popinées sitting around a fire. He gave them some fish and stayed to chat with them for a while. During this time, he managed to make a few furtive glances in the direction of his little girlfriend who was in the group. By bending down near her to pick up a piece of sugar cane (which he didn't need at all), he whispered a few words in her ear. He then got straight up and left, pretending to chew voraciously on the sugar cane.

He joined a group of Kanaks and spoke about forthcoming harvests. Next, he ate and busied himself with his daily chores. When night came, he went to bed and seemed to fall into a deep sleep – with his terrible club next to him, his knife in his belt and a spear within reach. When, in the great calm of the night, he could hear only the usual noises – the monotonous chirping of crickets, the moan of the wind in the leaves, the sound of the sea beating against the rocks, the heavy flight of some nocturnal bird of prey – once he was certain, by listening to the breathing coming from neighbouring huts, that the Kanaks were asleep, he gathered up his weapons, crawled out of his hut, moved slowly away and stopped to listen. Then he crept out, careful not to let any dry twigs crack underfoot. He got to the bush, stood up and continued, silently pushing on further into the forest. He stopped occasionally to listen out for any danger.

M'Baraï slowly poked his head out of the bushes and looked at the beach that stretched out clear and quiet under the radiant stars. He lay down in the grass and tried to make sense of what he was seeing – the swaying shrubbery, the dead wood lying on the ground, the recesses in the sand, the bobbing shadows, the broken tree trunk standing up, unmoving… all of these undefinable visions, mystified by the night, were suspicious.

After observing the scene and not noticing anything unusual, M'Baraï went down to the beach, walking backwards until he was in the sea. He then began walking on tiptoe, taking long strides. He took off, like a shadow, running the whole length of the beach without leaving the water and without making a splash.

He got to the dugout canoes that were floating, immobile, like big sleeping lizards. He untied one and got in, standing up at the back. A pole rose up over M'Baraï before it leaned forward and the dugout began sliding through the sea, long and silent, puckering the dark water as it went. It was going towards a head of rocks jutting out into the sea a short distance away.

Before it reached the rocks, a black, human shape broke away from the darkness, moved through the water, and waited. The dugout picked it up as it passed and headed out to sea. When the pole no longer touched the bottom, the silhouette and the half-caste both started paddling, moving further away from the coast.

M'Baraï was leaving Malekula where death had spared him several times but was no longer willing to show him mercy. He was fleeing death, taking with him his young popinée, who had followed him willingly.

XII

The casting off was guided by short, guttural commands in English. The pulleys squealed as they turned. They were accompanied by the sailors' voices and the sound of bare feet slapping the deck in rhythm. The windlass pounded the deck with its resounding blows and the chain grated in its hawes pipe. The jibs climbed jerkily up the stays, making a metallic clicking sound, and there were a few dull thuds as the canvas caught the wind. The ship yawed, raised its topsail, unfurled its staysail ropes, pitched in the breeze and made sail towards the savage islands.

Then it was the water hammer of the waves that broke on the glinting bow and the gentle skimming of the water along the side of the ship. Jean M'Baraï heard all of this from the ship's hold - as he was in the hold, along with a hundred or so Kanakas from different islands in the archipelago of the New Hebrides.

The half-caste athlete was wearing a pair of blue cotton pants that were too tight for him and a red striped Oxford shirt that he had draped over his shoulders as he couldn't put it on without busting the seams. For his personal use, he had been given a plate, a spoon and a pitcher – all of which were made of wrought iron – but they had taken his knife away. He had also been given a coarse little grey blanket. A tin medal marked with the number 96 had been hung on a knotted string around his powerful neck.

Running lengthways on either side of the hold were planks of wood that were stacked one upon the other like shelves. These served as camp beds for the niggers. M'Baraï had his place there. A large open panel provided ventilation as well as a view of a patch of sky and part of the sails billowing in the wind. In a far corner, there was a bucket for their excrement. In another corner there was a barrel on its side, containing drinking water, with an opening on top to allow them to fill their pitchers. Packed in like livestock, the Kanakas, who were apathetic by nature, spent most of their time sleeping. Or else they stayed lying down to kill time. They only got up to eat – any time of the day or night.

A few groups of creatures, stunned and groggy by the incessant pitching and brutal conditions of the slave ship, dressed in a disparate fashion in clothes that still had their labels in but were already soiled, clothes that they had put on without really knowing how or where to put them, were squatting around a metal bucket. They were there to eat and thus keep their minds occupied. They were beast-like beings, a coppery-black colour with strong jaws, flat noses and darting eyes (for they were instinctively cagey), with thoughts only for the grub in front of them. Every so often, a hand would shoot out, plunge into the bucket, emerge full of rice and discharge its load into a lapping, voracious mouth. One of the creatures would get up, with some difficulty, groaning, and would go and lie back down in his place. He would be replaced by another one. And so on and so on.

The Kanakas were from different islands or from neighbouring tribes that had been long-time enemies. They did not know each other and remained wary. They observed each other slyly, like animals of different species locked up together in a cage. Those who were from the same area and who spoke the same language stuck together, by tacit agreement, so they could defend themselves against the others if the need arose. The Kanakas did not talk… Occasionally, a few fearful whispers could be heard.

In the interests of hygiene (and to ensure the slave traders a profit), once a day, on a rotating basis and with rifles trained on them, twenty or so Kanakas were taken up on deck to get some fresh air and sunshine. They would sit or lie down, indifferent to their surroundings, looking at neither the sea nor the panoramic view of the islands. None of it mattered to them - as it wasn't home.

A bunch of Kanakas descended into the dark depths of the hold. Another ascended – M'Baraï was among them. The half-caste stood, leaning on the rail, watching the waves that were breaking on the bow. Then he cast his eyes towards the stern. He saw, squatting on the poop deck, a group of popinées – his popinée was with them. All of the women were dressed in gaudy printed calico smocks. The young popinée looked at her half-caste and signalled for him to come. With this, M'Baraï started off towards the stern of the ship but he was stopped in his tracks by a rifle barrel that was pointed at his chest and he was forced to turn back.

When he was back on the forward deck, the half-caste wanted to explain, in his own language, to defend his rights. He spoke in the Kanak language of Malekula mixed with a few words of French and a bit of bichelamar, which took a while to come out. The Englishmen didn't listen to him. Instead, to calm him down, they gave him a pipe and a good supply of tobacco.

M'Baraï, who hadn't smoked for more than four years, took great pleasure in it as it dulled his pain, improved his ability to think and even inspired him to philosophise. After all, even if they had taken his woman, he was better off here on board the ship than in the Malekulan tribe where they wanted to kill him and eat him. Obviously, he was no longer a bosun but he had escaped and was alive and well. All he needed to do now was to remain docile and patient.

His thoughts then turned to his Kanak wives who he had married according to Kanak custom. He was unmoved. He remembered his departure with the young popinée in the dugout canoe and his arrival alongside the silent ship that outlined his black silhouette against the clear night sky and whose slender masts scraped the stars. He had called out. Shadowy figures leaned over the railings and a ladder was lowered. M'Baraï had at that point thought that they were going to welcome him aboard like a fellow sailor in distress, a brother upon whom misfortune had fallen. He was the first to scale the ladder. His popinée followed. As soon as he had clambered on deck, he was kept at bay at gunpoint and had not been allowed to speak. The English sailors took he and his popinée to the foot of a mast and sat them down against a case of water. They were kept there until the captain woke up the next morning.

When the authorities on board the ship saw him, he had wanted to tell them his story, tell them that he was a half-caste from New Caledonia, a shipwrecked sailor. Even though he had doubtlessly explained it badly, the English recruiters had understood him – he was sure of that. But they made out that they had no idea what he was trying to say.

This strong man with the bronzed complexion – half-caste or no half-caste – was a fine catch. He was worth forty pounds sterling, maybe more. And the popinée who was of sound constitution too would bring at least half of that sum. It was a good bit of business.

After this summary judgement, the sailors took his knife and cast his canoe adrift. Then they ordered him to go down into the hold. In view of their threats (and out of respect for this kind of discipline that he had known when he was a sailor), he obeyed.

When he arrived at the bottom of the hold, he realised that his popinée had not followed him. His past life as a recruiter suddenly flashed before his eyes and he saw red. Did the English slavers behave the same way as the French and slavers of other nationalities? He smashed his fist into his palm with rage, unable to protest in any other way.

He had been on board with the Kanakas for four days – fed, dressed and treated like them – he, M'Baraï, a half-caste. Other Kanakas, new ones, had been thrown, stunned and dazed, into the hold. They were from the North of Malekula. M'Baraï had spoken with them: these Kanakas had been captured during warfare with enemy Kanaks. Instead of killing them, the victors preferred to exchange them with the slave traders for rifles and ammunition.

This deal had been brokered and closed from a distance. A crowd of Kanaks had made signals to the slavers and then waited patiently on the beach.

The slave traders' two whaleboats had come about 50 metres from the coast. They stopped there, turned around and started to back towards the shore. Then one of them came to a halt and held off. The men in this boat each took a rifle and kept close watch on the islanders' movements. The other whaleboat continued backing until it was almost touching the beach with its rear. It stayed there, its bow pointing out to sea, its crew holding onto the oars, ready to heave ho and away. The men who were not rowing aimed their rifles at the men on land, fingers on triggers.

As the whaleboats approached, most of the natives took off to the bushes surrounding the beach. Some of them waited on the beach to negotiate. Words spoken in bichelamar were exchanged at 20 paces. The deal was made.

The negotiators retreated to the bushes. Protected vigilantly by his fellow slavers who watched every move, one of the men got out of the whaleboat and placed a rifle on the sand. Immediately, two niggers with their hands tied together came out from behind a shrub and waded into the water until it was waist-deep.

They were hauled by the arms into the whaleboat. They seemed overjoyed. In the meantime, a native had picked up the rifle on the beach. The man from the whaleboat lay another rifle down in the same place and two more niggers with their hands tied emerged. And so the trade continued until seven rifles and fourteen niggers had changed hands. Next, the cartridges were thrown on the ground from afar.

Once the trading had finished and the whaleboats were rowing away from the beach, gunshots were fired from the bushes. Bullets whistled and ricocheted off the water. A rower slumped forward, wounded in the stomach. The boats returned fire, in a volley of shots, as the rowers pulled forcefully on the oars to make their escape… This is what the Malekulan Kanakas had told M'Baraï.

While he was under the inspirational spell of the tobacco and was lost in all these thoughts that were very arduous for him, the sailors ordered the Kanakas to go back down into the hold. The half-caste followed them.

In spite of having his pipe (that was often lit), down in the hold the days went by, one after the next, unchanging and depressing - he ate at designated times, and ate again between meals to finish off the leftovers. The only form of entertainment came in the shape of the two hours per day that were spent on deck.

The English schooner recruited for another month in the islands. When it had a full load of blacks, it flew the English flag, left the archipelago and took to the open sea, its bow ploughing forcefully through the great blue swells of the Pacific Ocean.

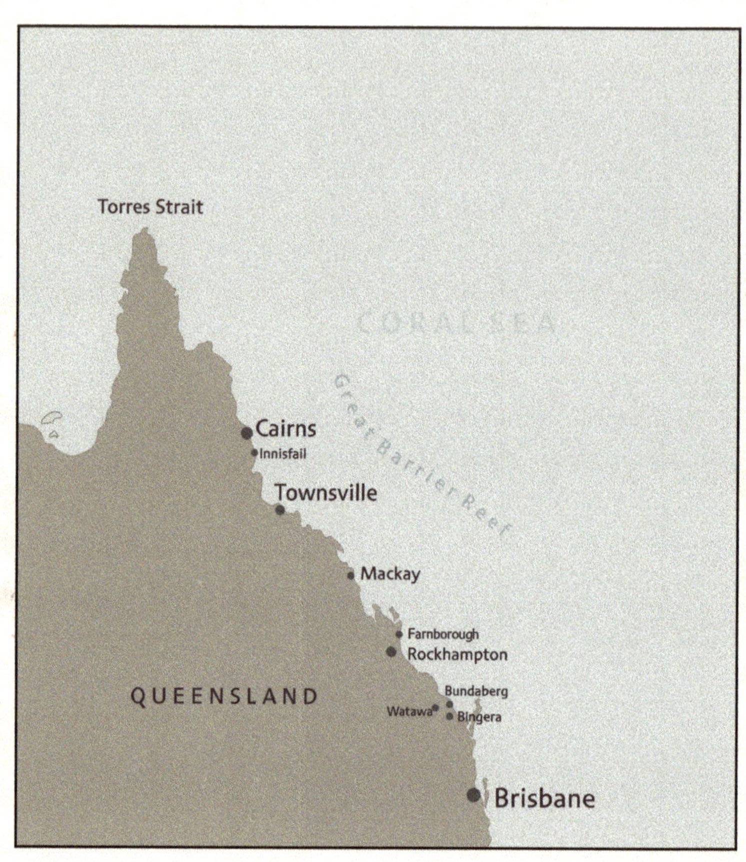
Torres Strait
CORAL SEA
Great Barrier Reef
Cairns
Innisfail
Townsville
Mackay
Farnborough
Rockhampton
QUEENSLAND
Bundaberg
Watawa
Bingera
Brisbane

PART THREE

I

On the deck of the schooner, the Kanakas, stunned and senseless from the voyage, awkward in their European clothes, were squeezed up close together like livestock. Tribal origins were no longer a distinguishing factor. Now they were simply all blacks at the mercy of the whites. Taut ropes marked out the limits that they could not pass. They were no longer surrounded by armed guards. The slave traders on board the ship moved them around, addressing them in paternal tones.

Rows of white men's huts stretched out before the eyes of the Kanakas. There were high walls pierced with holes, one above the next – they understood the purpose of these holes as they noticed heads and bodies going through them. There was smoke everywhere, like on the volcano on Ambrym. In some places smoke was coming out of pipes, like on boats propelled by fire. There were a lot of white men on land, all wearing clothes. They were walking about with their arms dangling at their sides, carrying neither spears nor rifles. Some of them were wearing manous like the popinées on the ship – they looked like wide pants with only one leg... maybe these were the white men's popinées.[65] Then there were some huge beasts that they had never seen before – much bigger than porkers. They were attached to things that rolled - kind of like the logs they used to drag their dugout canoes along.

All of these men and beasts were walking along tracks as wide as the sand at low tide. There were no trees, no lianas, no bush – nothing but big huts on either side of the tracks. This tribe of white men made sounds like the waves on pebbles. In the water, there were boats and more boats – some whistled like the wind in the coconut trees during a cyclone.

It was too much all at once for these Kanakas from the islands. They didn't even try to understand. These were white men's things, which are not the same as black men's things - that was all. With this mentality, once the initial surprise had passed, they reverted back to their natural state of indifference for anything that was not directly related to them. They looked on without seeing.

---

65 A "manou" is a Polynesian (Wallisian) word used in New Caledonia to describe the length of cloth worn wrapped around the body like a Samoan "lava-lava".

Jean M'Baraï the half-caste stood slightly apart from the mass of niggers. He was not indifferent to all the things he was seeing, he understood them, realising that this place was bigger and more beautiful than Noumea, that it was like what he'd seen in the pictures in books. He didn't know how to read, but he liked looking at the pictures… after he'd turned them over several times to find the right way up.

In his depressed state, a state brought on by the long stay amongst the savages of Malekula and then by his treatment as a prisoner aboard the ship, the half-caste could no longer think. He accepted his position as an inferior being, as a nigger for sale, without even contemplating that things could be any other way. The mental insensitivity of the New Caledonian Kanak came back out in him.

A small runabout sidled up to the ship. Some gentlemen climbed aboard and the captain and his mates welcomed them. While this was happening, the sailors gently organised the Kanakas into several lines.

The gentlemen walked up and down the rows of Kanakas, feeling the merchandise, making the niggers open their mouths and stick out their tongues. They jotted down in little notebooks the numbers on the tin medals hanging around the Kanakas' necks. Sometimes they showed more interest in certain individuals – they looked at them from all angles, examined them, then either left them in their row or pulled them out into another group apart from the rest.

They stopped in front of M'Baraï, saw that he was the strongest of them all and decided he must have been of Maori stock. They felt his muscles, thumped his bulging chest and told him to walk and do a twirl. Satisfied with his anatomy, they said, "*Good boy*", then sent him back to his row. Throughout this inspection, the very docile half-caste didn't say a word.

These activities went on for a very long time. After inspecting the popinées, the gentlemen left. They were from the Health Department and Customs, officials responsible for the reception of the niggers and for ensuring that their contracts conformed to the established laws.

Immediately following their departure and once the order of free circulation had been given, the Queensland buyers came aboard to make their selections and haggle over the prices of the niggers. They strutted about, important and superior, eying up the men for sale. Like connoisseurs, they studied the merchandise on the hoof. In order to judge their strength and resistance, they shook, pushed and hit the cowering blacks hard on the shoulders. The blacks understood nothing of this jostling.

The price for ordinary niggers had been set in advance – it was *thirty pounds each*. Ordinary looking niggers were grouped in packs and deals were made.

A tall Englishman with broad, square shoulders and a bushy bottlebrush moustache that covered his mouth, grabbed M'Baraï by the arm with his enormous hand and went to shake him. The stocky half-caste contracted his muscles, held himself steady, putting all his weight on his athletic legs, and stood there, unmoving, like a rock. The Englishman was very satisfied – he had to have this *nigga*. He spoke to the vendors.

There was competition, however, and the starting bid rose to forty pounds. The other buyers looked at the subject and studied his performance. And the auction began. The *bids* went up, pound by pound… until it was all done, all finished, everyone was silent… the *nigga* of Malekula, M'Baraï, was sold to Sir Wentworth Ramsbottom for the sum of *fifty-six pounds*. This gentleman was the Englishman with the bottlebrush moustache – the half-caste belonged to him for five years.

An agent of Sir Wentworth Ramsbottom added the half-caste to the group of twenty-five niggers he was looking after. Then, led by the agent, the herd of blacks with fuzzy hair, dazed by the movement of the traffic and the people, traipsed barefoot through the Brisbane streets, each man lugging a poorly rolled up blanket. The herd entered a courtyard and from there they moved into a room surrounded by offices and counters. An order was given and the niggers got undressed, ready for the anthropometric assessment. When they got to the height gauge, they obstinately lowered their heads, as they feared they would be hit. With great difficulty, the white men managed to get the blacks to tell them their island and tribe of origin and their Kanak name. To this they added an English name and a number.

When it was M'Baraï's turn, he wanted to explain that he was from New Caledonia. Whether they understood him or not, it made no difference – he had been recruited in Malekula so he was from Malekula. They wrote in his indenture papers: *"M'Baraï Peter from Malekula No. 7643. Claims to have worked in New Caledonia."*

Once these formalities were over, the group, still led by the agent, headed for the station. On the way, they stopped in the street, on the kerb, in front of a *shop*, to buy bully beef and ship's biscuit. Then they continued on their way. They arrived at the station and the blacks were herded into a cattle wagon where they all stood so they could see out. A sudden, piercing whistle made them all jump. The train moved off, leaving with a clang, frightening the niggers who, shaken and tossed around by the wagon in motion, began involuntarily dancing the pilou. They all clung on to the wooden bars that went around the top of the wagon. But, after a while, they got used to this new regime and were no longer scared.

Houses flashed past the eyes of the niggers in the wagon, then gardens, grasslands, trees… from time to time lone houses, isolated in the countryside, and bridges that rolled like thunder… and black holes where, out of fright, they ducked their heads, swallowing smoke and getting grit in their eyes. Finally, they saw only straight trees that all seemed to be the same. Sometimes the train stopped, people bustled about in a shed, and the train would leave again.

And then it was night and the Kanakas couldn't see anything anymore so they sat and lay down at the far end of the wagon, which, with its little bumps and jerks, kept shifting them towards the back.

It had been dark for a really long time and the stars were twinkling above the niggers. A long whistle was heard and the train slowed down before coming to a gentle stop. A man carrying a lantern came to the niggers' wagon at the end of the line and told them to get out. They did so with their numb legs, stumbling and hurting their feet on the ballast, the rails and the railway sleepers – none of which they had any knowledge of. They followed the man with the lantern and gathered in a shed.

After a moment's rest, the man with the light put the niggers on a cart track. He extinguished his lantern and gave the "black-fellows" the order to walk in front of him, following the road. They did this promptly as none of the Kanakas wanted to stay near the horse as it frightened them. Despite the blackness of the night, they took off at a fine pace so they wouldn't be bitten in the back by the big beast.

At the crack of dawn, they arrived at their destination, were straight away housed in a big wooden shack surrounded by other similar shacks. All of the Kanakas, who were tired from the upheaval of their journey and the long walk, fell asleep, each man in a wooden bunk stuffed with straw.

II

Six months had passed since the arrival of Peter M'Baraï at the homestead of the landlord who grew sugar cane and corn. If the discipline was very severe, if the niggers were sometimes punched or thrashed with bullwhips, there were some advantages – the food was abundant and sound, and hygiene was rigorously observed. Two hundred niggers lived in this establishment. Once a week, on Saturday, under the watchful eye of the foremen, they were forced to wash in pools, to soap each other up and change into clean clothes. These Kanakas received a wage of ten shillings per month. They were there to become civilised and not to make their fortunes.

The half-caste's robustness saw him employed as a tree feller. He cut trees to clear the land and prepare it for planting. This work required a whole lot of gear – saws, axes, jacks, ropes – which reminded M'Baraï of the operations he'd carried out on board ships. For this reason, M'Baraï enjoyed this activity, especially when a giant tree fell down, crushing its smaller neighbours.

The only inconvenience of the job was that he had to watch out for the numerous snakes that lived in these forests. To protect themselves from this danger, all the men, white and black who were employed to clear the land, wore strong hobnail shoes and leather leg protectors. Despite these precautions, a Kanaka that had been bitten on the hand by a little snake, had died a few minutes later. And these "men-Island" were really scared of these creatures who could "kill me fellow". When they found a snake, they all got together to step on it and squash it. They had great respect for a certain bird – the Jackass – as they had been told these birds killed snakes. They called the Jackass the "comrade belong man".

In addition to working and keeping clean, there was also the matter of spiritual care. On Sunday mornings, a missionary in a long, black frock coat, accompanied by a few English employees of the establishment who were rigid and serious for the occasion, gathered the niggers together in a big farm shed. There the pastor read them passages from the bible and gave them explanations. The blacks seemed attentive but only listened with half an ear to these monotonous words that told stories that made no sense at all to them. The valorous clergyman did his utmost to teach them the psalms, but the "men belong islands", in spite of their best efforts (made mostly to avoid being manhandled), were not very gifted for liturgical chants. They brayed in chorus without being able to fathom the usefulness of this additional work.

In the afternoon, the niggers were allowed to walk around freely. They preferred going far from their residence, far from the eyes of the masters, to certain places where they could procure cheap gin. Then they partook in drinking bouts and binges followed by fights amongst themselves. In the night, they returned to their camp, grouping themselves by islands, in a touching kind of solidarity, some of them pulling their mates along or even carrying those who were dead drunk. The following day at work, they'd already be thinking about the next Sunday when they would start the party over again.

Most of these niggers had consented to leave their islands to work for the whites with the sole intention of drinking alcohol to purposely get drunk. That was all that they found good about civilisation.

Some Sundays when Sir Wentworth Ramsbottom was *at home*, when he felt the need to relax or he wanted to treat some visitors, he would give the order to bring ten or so selected niggers to him. The Kanakas were led out onto the lawn in front of the pleasant, planter's cottage. He and his guests waited under the veranda, all comfortably installed in rocking chairs with their feet up. They had either a cigar or a pipe in their mouths (depending on availability) and some whisky *of best quality* at close hand.

Several employees of the establishment, Jim, Sam, Bob and Pat, took care of the formalities of the ceremony. Two niggers' black hands were put into voluminous gloves that were tied at their wrists. The two blacks were there, clumsy and oafish, with their arms arched widely out from their bodies, weighed down by the heavy round pads that hung from their extremities. The managers sat the two Kanakas down on a chair each, a few paces apart, next to a bucket in which a stable sponge was floating. Then they explained the sacred rules of the noble sport of boxing to them.

When the final recommendations had been made, Sir Ramsbottom, let fly an energetic "*Go ahead*". The two well-trained niggers got up, stepped forward, awkwardly gave each other a few gloved punches before retreating a few steps back. Another order came and they flew at each other like brutes, without thinking, hitting randomly at their opponent's face or into the air. The first one to be really put in his place drew away without stopping, protecting his eyes with his forearms, pulling his head down into his shoulders and arching his back. When a nose or a mouth bled, it was to the great delight of the crowd of gentlemen, who encouraged the champions, gesticulating and shouting, "*Give it to him!*"

It was at this point that they raised the bets. They'd stop the fight for a few minutes to wipe off the blood and let the champions get their breath back. Then it would start again. When the referees judged that a competitor had had enough, that he was knocked senseless enough that he was no longer of any interest, they would move on to the next match and so it would go on. Sunday afternoon would pass like this, quietly, doing sport, far away from the intellectual concerns of business.

III

The number one black boxer on Sir Ramsbottom's plantation was Peter M'Baraï. As soon as they had tried his worth at this art, he displayed his innate qualities. Without any training in this sport (aside from beating up Kanakas), he had some natural talents that gave him an unquestionable advantage – he was tough, stubborn as a mule, could receive blows almost without flinching and when he landed a good punch, he would nearly always knock his opponent out cold. M'Baraï was too physically strong to fight *niggers*. Moreover, he enjoyed the prestige that came with being a half-caste – the Kanakas feared him – which also gave him a huge psychological advantage over his adversaries. A few blacks from neighbouring properties had fought against him, but with no success. For these reasons, M'Baraï's fights no longer held any interest, as there was no competition.

On the occasion of a *holiday*, Sir Wentworth Ramsbottom Esq. managed to overcome the repugnance Englishmen feel about fighting blacks, unless, of course, they are beating them to punish them. Pat the *ploughman*, a tall red-headed Irishman, agreed to fight M'Baraï, in return for the sum of four pounds sterling, with an extra six pounds should he win the bout.

Pat had done a bit of boxing as, although he was a labourer, he was ambitious. He wanted to be a policeman. This was a condition set by Daisy if she were to become "*his wife*". But "*poor Pat*" was unlucky. Each time he had gone to Brisbane to ask for a job at the Police Department, he had firstly wasted his money and then had been picked up for his intemperance. For this reason, his admission had always been deferred. Persevering in his hope to marry Daisy, he enrolled himself in a temperance society so he could correct his prejudicial affliction. But it was in vain, and worst of all, when he promised he'd no longer touch whisky, he found it even more tempting and went back to the bars trying to pass unnoticed. This was Pat's situation when his meeting with Peter M'Baraï the *woodcutter* was decided.

On a sunny afternoon, before a select crowd, "*the gentry of the Country*", on the freshly cut lawn assigned to the fight, the match between Pat "*the Irish*" and Peter M'Baraï "*the black fellow*" took place.

Seeing himself in the presence of an opponent who seemed formidable, as he had learned to box, M'Baraï sensed that he would not be as easy to beat as a Kanaka. This thought made him solemn and nasty. He had no idea of sportsmanship - he thought only of hurting this big man who wanted to beat him up.

As for Pat, he didn't have much regard for this "black fellow" who wasn't "*scientific*". He merely saw it as his duty to beat him, without malice or anger, to win six pounds sterling so he could buy Daisy a gold brooch in the shape of the Australian continent with a little Tasmania pendant hanging below.

The lead-up to the fight took place according to usual practice then the opponents got straight down to business. M'Baraï rushed right at big Pat with his head down, punching as he advanced without worrying about protecting himself from any blows. The heavy and brutal thrust of the half-caste forced the Irishman backwards, who all the while kept punching his attacker's head - M'Baraï didn't seem to feel the punches, taking no notice of them. Pat was finding it really hard to breathe with the onslaught of punches to his chest. When the end of the first round was announced, M'Baraï wanted to continue getting stuck into his opponent but the assistants and Sir Ramsbottom himself intervened immediately. In the presence of the master, the enraged half-caste restrained himself.

When the match resumed, M'Baraï went back to pounding his adversary. The blows that the Irishman dealt him didn't seem to trouble him at all, he continued advancing, never staggering, pulling his head in like a turtle. At one point, the half-caste punched his adversary hard in the guts, he collapsed, his breathing cut off. It took several minutes before he came round.

The experts decided that Pat was the winner on points and, if Peter M'Baraï had the knock out, it was because he didn't know how to box according to the rules. Despite this, in all fairness, the prize was shared between the two champions.

Then these gentlemen, these sportsmen, examined Peter M'Baraï more closely. They squeezed his muscles to check their firmness. They made him run around a field, timing his run. They took note of his breathing and his heart rate. After a short break, they made him jump over a wooden pole that they gradually lifted higher and higher. When they had studied the half-caste's performances like horse dealers study those of a horse, they agreed that this "black fellow" was worth good money.

This syndicate of gentlemen took Peter M'Baraï into their charge to teach him the science of boxing, train him and then put him into the ring. They did so without asking him what he thought about it, persuaded that this *nigger* was very flattered to receive such a great honour.

A few days after being examined by this learned assembly, Peter M'Baraï was dressed in new clothes, Englishmen's clothes. Never had he been so well turned out in his life. He was taken to Brisbane to a teacher's house. He was a sort of gladiator trainer who taught boxing and educated and trained his charges in useful subjects, according to the classical method. M'Baraï was the only student who lived-in. He was extremely bored there.

Then the training started. The half-caste was put on a special diet and his private life was rigorously supervised, just like an animal whose life no longer belonged to him. In the morning, he was dressed in flannel. Then, under the watchful eye of his trainer, he did gymnastics in a public park. Sometimes, a few women walking in the park, partial to animalistic sensations, smiled at him invitingly. They could tell by the exercises he was doing that this tanned chap was a boxer, an all-round athlete, "don't you think?"… "None of that please, Lisette…" Led away by his mahout, Peter M'Baraï was taken back to his stall, before being washed, sponged, massaged and put to bed. So that he couldn't waste his energy on anything that wasn't productive for the syndicate, he was never allowed out on his own.

After a light meal, he did some weightlifting. Then, he drove his fists into a punching ball, learning to move his head quickly to the side to avoid the fast returning ball. This exercise lasted for an hour with a few moments' break.

In the afternoon, a boxing teacher taught him the subtleties and finer points of this energetic science. As M'Baraï had the aptitude, he made quick progress. To familiarise M'Baraï with the audience, develop a taste for the noble sport in him and arouse his emulation, his manager would often taken him out of an evening to watch the boxing matches in a local hall. He'd leave overexcited and wanting to smash his fist in someone's face. He was taken back to bed in a sort of cell that they locked to stop him from running off and losing the fruit of his methodical training.

Sometimes his trainer would organise training matches with second-rate boxers to see how his pupil was going. Peter M'Baraï had size, dexterity, hand-eye coordination and speed but he lacked composure. When the fight heated up, he got angry and wasted his strength. It was very bad for a professional boxer.

After six months of this measured and rational training, when the half-caste was really fit, after the preliminary challenges launched via the press, after much hype that M'Baraï knew nothing about, posters appeared, stuck up on walls, announcing a big boxing match between "*Peter M'Baraï, the Maori*" and "*Jack Nottingham the Champion of Rockhampton*".

Before the match, the group of syndicate shareholders, with Sir Wentworth Ramsbottom at the head, gave their final recommendations to Peter M'Baraï and shook him firmly by the hand, for he represented the honour of the Country planters.[66]

With his broad shoulders, confident air, bulging muscles chiselled from copper, wearing a red costume with a black scarf and with his big, woolly head on his shoulders, Peter M'Baraï seemed the picture of conscious strength and composure, reminiscent of an ancient gladiator born under the African sun.

When, blinded by the light, he was taken into the ring, he could only see mountains of heads around him that rose in terraces and could only feel the thousands of eyes that were boring into him. He lost his bearings. While they were putting on his gloves, he heard the jibes of the *larrikins*. They were making fun of him, which ended up making him lose concentration. Without understanding it, he was being subjected to the nasty power of a

---

66   'Country planters' here most likely means plantation owners of inland and northern Queensland who utilized Kanak labour and became a significant political voice in Queensland.

crowd because he wasn't white and wasn't Australian.

His adversary had a dark complexion, was the same weight as him but was taller and more svelte. He was an Australian. They did the boxer's handshake that preceded the fight and the attack began – calm and clever in Jack's corner.

Peter M'Baraï lacked sang-froid. He fought without thinking, without planning his moves and without conserving his force. The shouting and name-calling coming from the crowd – "*Go on, Blackie! Get to him Nigger! Go it Sambo! I bet on the Darkie!*" – further contributed to his dazed state. His frame of mind became that of a bull that had been baited in an arena – he no longer knew what he was doing there and he floundered about. His opponent landed a direct hit that mashed his lips into his teeth and blood streamed out of his mouth. Peter M'Baraï went crazy. He rushed towards Jack, who deftly avoided his blows. But the half-caste caught him, seized him around the waist, twisted his back, threw him on the ground and began to pummel him. It was against the laws of boxing and the assistants intervened immediately. Peter M'Baraï, fierce and determined as a bulldog, didn't want to let go. Some professionals leapt over the ropes. The half-caste, who didn't understand anything anymore, defended himself as if the men were wanting to kill him – he must have thought he was back on Malekula Island. To remind him of the conventions of the sport, the boxing professionals bashed him senseless. He was knocked out.

While this was happening, Jack Nottingham, who had extricated himself from the scrum, sat down very calmly on his folding chair with his legs stretched out, his arms resting on the ropes and he let his team fan him with a towel and massage his limbs so he would be ready for the next bout.

When Peter M'Baraï came to, he learned that he had been disqualified. His furious impresario put him in a *cab* and took him *home* where he put him back under lock and key.

The *nigger* Peter M'Baraï had let the syndicate down. His education and training had cost a lot of money, all the bets placed on him had been lost and the honour of the *Country* had been compromised. Since he had not been able to manage his violent character, he was a worthless man for whom they no longer had any consideration. They had given him the opportunity to become someone famous, to go to England or America but he hadn't been able to capitalise on this and was thus not worth their interest.

And so ended the boxing career of the New Caledonian half-caste Jean M'Baraï…

Despite his goodwill, the half-caste had been unable to vanquish his heredity - whether he was giving or receiving blows, he always got angry - as was the nature of his race. He wasn't made for sport. Words spoken firmly and without violence could dominate him… but brutality made him into a savage beast.

IV

Poor Peter M'Baraï was put back into the ranks with the same status as all the other *niggers*. He cut down many, many trees – as if he wanted to clear the whole of Queensland – without anyone really paying any attention to him. Despised by the English since his fall from grace, all that was left to him was the company of the blacks with whom he worked. With neither advice nor moral support from the whites, he became fully Kanak, took part in their pleasure and pain and contracted their habits of intemperance. He too waited for Sunday to go and drink and frequent a few poor wretches who stooped to that kind of clientele. Having both the taste and the training for it, Peter M'Baraï became a fighter when he was drunk. He had been arrested for fighting several times, spending days in jail and having to pay fines. The discouraged half-caste worked without passion, without initiative, unwillingly even, obeying orders like a beast of burden unconscious of his utility.

Everything that represented primitive Australia had long been pushed far from the region where M'Baraï was living. He never experienced what has become the classic cliché – Aborigines, boomerangs, kangaroos and emus. He did see, however, some of these marsupials and big birds locked up behind wire fences. He occasionally saw some Queensland half-castes, mostly vagrants, idlers, drunks and thieves. Aside from the flora, which he attacked with his axe, and the snakes and goannas that he squashed, he knew nothing of the country.

Despite being deadened by this depressing life, Jean M'Baraï held on to one thought, one single goal – he wanted to finish his five-year indenture, return to New Caledonia and go back to his father's place, his land. There he would go to ground near the sea, under the coconut palms, have a little boat, fish and never go out in search of adventures on the high seas again.

And so the years passed slowly, unchanging, one after the next. The half-caste made no effort to climb the social ladder to escape from his life as an inferior being. Finally, the hour of deliverance was upon him. He was offered six shillings per day to stay in the service of Sir Wentworth Ramsbottom Esq. But he would not have accepted to stay in Australia for all the money in the world. And this, despite the wise advice of the 'missionary' who explained to him all of the present advantages and future recompenses. Like all New Caledonians,

M'Baraï liked independence and freedom. He was quickly bored by well-ordered, rigid and repetitive work that forced people to stay in one place, being assiduous and punctual. His early life had instilled in him the apathy of the Melanesians. He preferred to follow his whims – work hard when he felt so inclined, wander and roam if he felt the need, or stay in bed and sleep when he felt overcome by pure, sweet laziness.

When he went back to the nigger office to sort out his affairs, he explained, after a fashion, that he was born in New Caledonia, that his father was white and that he wanted to return home to him. They listened to him complacently and flicked through the big registers. On his identity page he had been listed as coming from Malekula so he had to be repatriated to that island, they couldn't infringe the laws or change them just for him. M'Baraï told them that the people on the island wanted to kill him. These gentlemen were interested in his fate but could do nothing about it. They did, however, come up with a solution – he could simply stay in Queensland. Faced with this choice – either be killed on Malekula or stay in Queensland – M'Baraï opted for Malekula as the danger was not immediate. He was given his savings, which only came to *two pounds four shillings and nine pence* after five years of work. As a matter of fairness, they had deducted the costs of the *Police Court* and the fines for his public drunkenness and brawling. He bought a few personal effects, a pipe and some tobacco.

He was loaded onto a little schooner with sixty odd Kanakas from different islands. The schooner was heading for the New Hebrides archipelago.

Jean M'Baraï was happy to once again be at sea, to feel the powerful swells lift the ship, like a flimsy leaf. He watched on admiringly as the white sails filled in the breeze to sail away from the Australian coast. After a few days, all of these joys mixed with the fragrance of the ocean had transformed the half-caste. The torpor that had weighed upon him for years had dissipated. He had become what he once was – a sailor.

The discipline imposed upon the repatriated niggers was tolerant – they didn't want to spoil future recruitment of black workers. During the day, the Kanakas were allowed to walk about on deck (but couldn't go to the stern) or stay in the hold if they wished. The half-caste helped with the steerage. He even obtained, as a special favour, the permission to do a stint at the helm. All of these joys made him forget that he was going back to Malekula, which was still far off. He had plenty of time to think about that later.

One morning, dark mountains appeared through the fog on the horizon. Not long after, the outlines became more distinct. With all her sails unfurled, the ship advanced at a rapid pace, leaving behind her a long, foamy trail. At around midday, the ship was along the coast of Espiritu Santo, it bore away, rounded a cape, came back upwind, tacked around a bit and, in the middle of the night, dropped anchor in Big Bay.

The regulations (and the interests of the recruiters) required the Kanakas to be put ashore in their own territories, in their own tribes – in other words, each man was to be returned to his respective home. The Kanakas themselves pointed out from on board ship where exactly on the coast they wished to disembark. If they made a mistake, if they landed in a region that was not their own, even if it was near their homeland, things were settled straight away – they were killed, then eaten. It was certainly a very efficient process of assimilation. Consequently, Kanakas who preferred to retain their nationality, protested with great conviction when the men on the whaleboat wanted to drop them off at a place that was not exactly theirs.

Repatriated Kanakas, loaded up with packages and their little, bright red sea chests, were put ashore along the coast, in water up to their waists, witnessed by large numbers of islanders assembled on the beach. As soon as they were among their brethren, before they could go any further – on the beach itself – the chests were smashed, bundles were ripped open, and it was a rapacious, violent scramble for the spoils. In an instant, all the objects and rags were scattered and torn to pieces by the natives who had appropriated them, much to the vexation of the new arrivals who were powerless to react. It was the custom.

The ship spent several days along the coast of Santo, dropping off niggers at different places, trading with a few little coasters, adventurers of the islands. Once all of the Kanakas had been repatriated, she then began recruiting.

Whether it was through insouciance or mental laziness, not once did M'Baraï think that he might have been able to make an arrangement with the captain to change his landing place. Since the authorities in Brisbane had decided that he had to be put ashore on Malekula, he had concluded that no one else had the power to change this order - he considered it set in stone. In any case, he knew that all of the islands were dangerous and thus had no preference for one over another. He was waiting to see what would play out.

After a few days, the ship arrived along the coastline of Malekula. While niggers were being put ashore and sent home, the half-caste began to worry about his own fate. He didn't, however, talk about this with anyone. The following afternoon, the ship dropped anchor more or less in the same place where, five years earlier, M'Baraï had boarded the brig with his popinée at night, after having escaped in the dugout canoe.

The bosun asked him where he wanted to go ashore. M'Baraï replied that he didn't want to disembark – neither there nor anywhere else on Malekula as the Kanaks were going to eat him.

There were many explanations made. He had to be put ashore there as he had been taken from this spot. If the Kanaks killed him afterwards well, that was no longer the concern of the officers in charge of the ship. M'Baraï protested vigorously – it wasn't his country, etc., etc. The *bosun* threatened to throw him into the sea. In one leap, the half-caste grabbed an iron bar for a weapon and, like a wild man, backed up against the ship's rail and waited for the attack, ready to smash in some heads. If he was going to be killed, he preferred it to be on board the ship. Fortunately, the sailors did not react aggressively. M'Baraï obstinately remained on his guard but did not have the chance to commit any irreparable acts of violence.

Hearing a fight, the captain came out of his cabin and went to see what was going on and re-establish order if necessary. Still holding the iron bar, the half-caste told his story again – his country was New Caledonia, it was not Malekula, he had been shipwrecked there, his father was white, etc…

The captain thought for a moment before speaking calmly to the half-caste. "I cannot keep you on board, it is against regulations. You must go ashore on Malekula… But, I'm willing to make an exception for you. If you intend to stay on the ship, you may, if you sign a five-year indenture to work in Queensland. Until we reach Brisbane, you will work as a sailor to pay for your keep."

So, he wouldn't have to go ashore to the cannibals… Queensland was far away, the ship would remain cruising in the archipelago for a long time yet and, between now and then, he'd see. Jean M'Baraï accepted the offer.

Upon the captain's request and in the presence of the shipboard authorities, Peter M'Baraï drew, at the bottom of a sheet of paper, a large cross that contracted him to work for five years.

And the ship continued her *business* in the archipelago. Jean M'Baraï, the half-caste, worked with the crew, mostly employed as a rower on the small boats.

One day the ship entered a Sandwich Island bay. She saluted a schooner that was anchored there, raising her English flag three times up the gaff. The schooner responded politely by hoisting the French flag - and the relationship did not go any further. The English and French ships were competitors in the archipelago. Each one was trying to develop the influence of her nation and, in the interest of her own business, prevent the rival from draining the resources of the islands.

The two ships were anchored a mile away from each other and each one was kept busy with her own dealings, carried out by little boats that went to land. While rowing like a galley slave, without even making an effort and without tiring, M'Baraï planned his move, which was not very complicated. When the sun went down, the little boats stopped their to-ing and fro-ing and the crews got some rest.

At around 10 or 11pm that night, when silence reigned on board the ship, a furtive shadow popped up from a hatch, slipped along the deck towards the bow, scaled the railing, grabbed the hawse hole, clung on tightly and made its way along the chain to the anchor, lowered itself without making a noise into the water and then began to swim. It was M'Baraï making his escape, breaking his five-year indenture and renouncing the cross that marked his signature. Where was he going? Simple - to the French ship.

He had left most of his possessions behind, taking only a tiny packet fixed to his head, which contained his tobacco, pipe, matches and a blue silk blend scarf. M'Baraï was lightly dressed in dark clothes as he knew that sharks were able to see white from a great distance in the water. He also knew that they hesitated before biting into fabric when they do not see any flesh. Fish do not wear clothes, do they? He had a knife in a sheath on his belt to defend himself if one of these "*bloody pigs*" came to attack him.

Without hurrying or becoming alarmed, swimming like he was going for a dip on a sunny day, he made it to underneath the bowsprit of the French schooner, rose up in the water, lifted his arms, kicked his legs, grasped hold of the bobstay and climbed on board. So he wouldn't get cold in the night air, he holed up in the bow, against the forestay sail, and smoked his pipe, patiently awaiting daybreak.

At dawn, the cook lit his fire to make coffee for the officers and tea for the crew. M'Baraï recognized from the cook's physiognomy that he was a "Saouett".[67] This observation put him at ease. He approached the kitchen, leaned in the doorway, his wet clothes clinging to him, and did not say a word. The cook continued attending to his business, without even noticing that this individual was not from the shipboard. M'Baraï slowly entered the kitchen and went over to the furnace to dry himself. The cook, who had probably seen some tough nuts in his life – something that fostered a sense of altruism among the wretched – left him to make himself comfortable, only saying a few words to him in French, to which M'Baraï answered yes without having really understood.

And the ship came to life, sailors from the Loyalty Islands moved about on the deck, came to get their *tea*, stared at M'Baraï who they did not recognize but they didn't speak to him. Besides, what did it matter to them – there were never any surprises in the islands, you got used to anything. The cook, who was a good chap, gave a quarter-litre pitcher of tea and a piece of bread to his guest who took it eagerly, without saying thank you. What was the point?

The sun had come up. A dry and comforted M'Baraï didn't dare leave the kitchen for fear of being seen by the captain. In accordance with his usual state of mind, when he had to make a decision that was subordinate to the volition of the Europeans and he had no one to guide him, he hesitated, put it off and waited for events to put him in an irreversible position. Driven by his dull anger, he'd then become excessively tenacious and obstinate. All at once, M'Baraï was both very timid and too bold.

In this particular case, things happened very easily. The first mate did his round of inspection to see that everything was in order. He went to have a look in the kitchen and found a half-caste smoking a pipe. He looked at him, then questioned him in bichelamar.

"What name you make here? – You came belong where?"

Instead of answering the question, M'Baraï called out his interlocutor's name: "Louis Laurent".

The first mate recognized him straight away and said, "Jean M'Baraï! Think you finish dead long time? Now you come back, you all same devil. No gammon".[68]

Louis Laurent the first mate was also a half-caste. Both men had been brought up practically together. They had then seen each other again sailing in the islands. M'Baraï gave him a quick rundown of his adventures and how he came to be on board the French ship.

Louis Laurent found his story quite ordinary and not of much interest. M'Baraï thought so too. These unsophisticated characters were not very sensitive to repercussions and the life of a slaver hardened their natures. They went to see the captain to fill him in on the present circumstances. Louis Laurent felt especially pleased to be able to play a dirty trick on an

---

67   Baudoux footnotes this term as referring to a freed convict from the New Caledonian penal system.
68   No gammon = No lies.

English recruiting ship.

Since business had concluded in this bay, the captain decided that, in order to avoid any complications with the English boat, they would cast off as soon as the morning wind could be established. One hour later, the schooner weighed anchor and left for another island.

The schooner continued to cruise the archipelago, finished her *business* and headed for her home port, Noumea, where she arrived without any further incident.

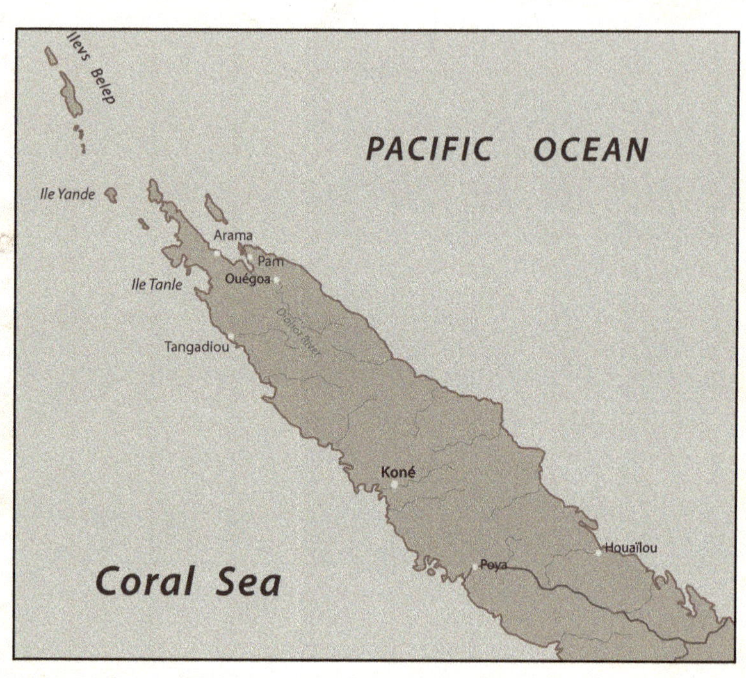

Ilevs Belep
Ile Yande
Ile Tanle
Arama
Pam
Ouégoa
Diahot River
Tangadiou
PACIFIC OCEAN
Koné
Houaïlou
Poya
Coral Sea

PART FOUR

I

A dozen years or so after his departure, like a homing pigeon returning to his dovecote, Jean M'Baraï returned to Tanlé…

When he arrived, he learned that his father had died a long time before. This unexpected news caused him pain, but that was not all. His grief turned to anger when, on the family property he found a Chinaman and a popinée, who was not his mother, living there. He wanted to forcibly evict them. After he dealt out a few blows, the Chinaman and his employees went to great lengths to calm him down. Then they explained themselves to him as best they could, in a sort of Esperanto… The Chinaman promised to leave the house after having referred the matter to the Administration, as he had been named custodian of the seals after the death of the owner. After that he had purchased the land. In order to ensure he'd be able to assert his rights, M'Baraï refused to leave. The Chinaman was obliged to temporarily come to an arrangement and allow M'Baraï to stay there, like it was his home.

But, shrewd diplomat that he was, all the while looking after M'Baraï so as not to get manhandled, the Chinaman approached the authorities. The Administrator in charge of Ouégoa had jurisdiction over the affair. At great expense, he sent a pair of gendarmes on horseback to Tanlé, recommending that they go to the aid of the Chinaman and, if necessary, seize the interloper to restore order to his arrondissement.

M'Baraï had instinctive respect for a uniform in general and irrational fear of the gendarme in particular. When he saw the two cops arriving, he lost all his fighting spirit.

Reinforced by a few neighbouring farmers who could serve as interpreters and possibly give the gendarmes a hand, the police sergeant with the big moustache acted in the capacity of temporary bailiff.

He explained to Jean M'Baraï, speaking to his person, "that his so-called father had not recognized him legally, that this surname M'Baraï was his mother's name, a Kanak woman from the Poya tribe, that consequently he did not have any right to claim the inheritance of the late X… that the trustee, after taking the usual steps, had every reason to believe that there was a claimant in Brittany and another who was supposedly residing in the Republic of Argentina. But that, at present, he, the police sergeant, acting in the capacity of bailiff, at the request of the Chinaman who was legally authorised, was informing him, Jean M'Baraï, that he could not under any circumstances remain on this property. In witness whereof, so that he could not claim he was unaware of it, he would leave him a copy of his writ, the cost of which was such and such."

Then, on a conciliatory note, to comfort the half-caste who was standing there with his mouth hanging open and his eyes wide, he added, "that he, Jean M'Baraï, could, as of this moment, if he had any claims to make, notify them or get them served by a bailiff and, in that event, seek advice from a lawyer to attack both the estate and the Chinaman."

The half-caste was dumbstruck at the flow of these words that were incoherent for him and he looked desperately around for someone there who could advise him or give him some moral support. Nobody moved, nobody dared to speak – they were afraid of compromising themselves.

The police sergeant, returning to his gendarme persona, adjusted his dolman, took in a deep breath of air, stuck out his chest, seemed to stretch up in height, and resumed in an authoritarian tone: "Jean M'Baraï, you have committed a serious offence in trespassing on the property of the Chinaman here present, and in assaulting him and his employees. Your offence is punishable under article X of the criminal code. In witness whereof, we, as uniformed police sergeants of the Gendarmerie, order you to vacate the property immediately. Should you refuse to obey our order, the plaintiff will uphold his complaint, you will be arrested and justice will follow its course." To persuade M'Baraï, he added, "And the Chinaman would also file a civil suit".

M'Baraï understood nothing of these words that were over his simple mental capacity, even when they were translated and explained. For that matter, the interpreters scarcely understood more than he. Stubborn and sticking to his story, he repeated in his language, "It's my father's land, *he* built the house, *he* planted the coconut palms, my mother helped him and so did I. My father told me that it would be mine when he died – that's always the way it is done, the land is for the children." He never let go of this reasoning, which at the heart of it was very logical.

Next, a hesitant M'Baraï tried to impose conditions. He would leave his father's land if the gendarmes gave him some land elsewhere so he could build a hut, plant some yams and live there.

Not wanting to get caught up in a messy situation, the police sergeant did not make any promises. He replied, "That is beyond the jurisdiction of the Gendarmerie, you will have to speak to the Land Office, they handle that type of request."

Then, using all the power of his voice, he reiterated his notice: "In the name of the law, Jean M'Baraï, will you, yes or no, leave this land that belongs to the Chinaman?" M'Baraï didn't move and remained mute.

In the presence of this apathetic resistance, the police sergeant, who knew only passive obedience, grew impatient. With a feverish hand, he stroked his handlebar moustache and thought for a few moments all the while shooting furious looks at M'Baraï. Then, he checked himself and became more accommodating. He knew this kind of uncooperative, stubborn type. He didn't want to have to drag a troublesome prisoner through the bush for a few days – a prisoner who could escape or lie on the ground and refuse to walk. He stalled by using bullying tactics.

"M'Baraï, be careful! You are making things worse for yourself! I am going to have to arrest you and put you in chains." And addressing his colleague he said, "We are going to arrest this delinquent. Get the handcuffs and chains ready!"

The cop pulled out chains, handcuffs and sparkling, polished steel thumbcuffs from a bulky bag he carried slung over his shoulder.

Seeing these instruments of torture, poor, distraught M'Baraï didn't even think of running. In the sea, he was not afraid of sharks, but on land he was afraid of horses, never having had much to do with them, especially not gendarmes' horses. Defeated, he mumbled in bichelamar: "Yes, me go now, ground here finish belong me." He picked up his few belongings and shuffled off with his head down, followed by the two gendarmes and the people who had come with them… The rule of law prevailed.

The poor devil walked slowly, carrying all his worldly possessions under his arm. Every now and then he would hit his tough and obtuse skull with his free hand, trying either to drum into it or extract from it an idea that would allow him to understand all of these things that were beyond his comprehension. They had stolen his land and his father's house, *his* land and *his* house, and they wanted to put *him* in chains to take *him* to the calabouse… Why? He could only see that an immense injustice had been meted out to him by the gendarmes and the bureaucrats from Ouéga who had taken the Chinaman's side – the Chinaman who was powerful as he had money.

After having threatened him with all the wrath of the justice system, and prison, and after having made him promise to behave himself, the gendarmes left M'Baraï in the Kanak tribe, where he found some of his childhood friends. He stayed there for a few days before leaving for the islands in the North to rejoin the half-castes he had known there in his youth.

The half-castes, who were always very hospitable, welcomed him warmly. He took up their occupations – copra and fishing – and settled in with them.

II

When the old Breton sailor had died, a smuggler from Yandé had plucked up his popinée, his legitimate widow, the mother of Jean M'Baraï. But he had an ulterior motive. He thought, without being absolutely sure, that as this popinée had lived with a white man as his wife and had contributed through her work in the creation of a communal property, there was every chance that it would remain hers. It could be through the right of occupancy – there had been several precedents of this along the coast. The popinée could also become the owner through inheritance, if the so-called husband had had the foresight to leave some kind of paper expressing this last wish.

This land planted with coconut palms was valuable. The smuggler fiercely defended the popinée's interests – interests that had also become his own. He paid for it out of his own pocket. On the insistence of several competitors, however, the property was put up for sale and auctioned off to the *Chinaman*.

Despite this great disappointment, the smuggler kept the popinée, who was already old but a very good woman and an excellent housewife – in a kind of rustic way. She lived quietly there, with the insensitivity and indifference that characterised the elderly people of her race.

Jean M'Baraï found his mother on this island. Their first meeting was very calm, unemotional and without any apparent displays of affection. They touched each other's hand, looking elsewhere, both uncomfortable to see each other again, to not recognize each other after so long a separation. They hardly spoke and did not mention the loss of the property. What was the point? It was a *fait accompli*. Then the old mama sat on a block of wood, silently smoked her narrow, dark pipe and looked at her son for hours. She followed him with her eyes, to get used to his presence, savouring her happiness without making it obvious to anyone.

Perhaps there was also a touch of superstition. Was her son a ghost? Sometimes, when he came close to her, to make sure it was really him, she touched him and would say "Bouaama Chean" (expression of pity meaning something like "Poor Jean"). And both of their lives went back to normal.

III

Jean M'Baraï continued to fish with his island friends. They were very good people, austere and sober, but perhaps just a bit too puritanical. They had been brought up by English people, who were more or less Mormons, and who had done their utmost to instil a puritan mentality and develop a real sense of thine and mine in them. In the evenings, they would read the Bible to each other, taking pleasure in commenting on and interpreting the most suggestive passages.

During his long absence of twelve or more years, it was clear that M'Baraï had had some adventures, as he had adopted some very bad manners. Now he was no longer a good boy. Jean M'Baraï liked alcohol and he looked for opportunities to drink. But he did more than drink – he got drunk. Yes, he got drunk! When he was inebriated, he become really unpleasant, as he was a sad drunk who talked too much. M'Baraï told stories, extraordinary things, sometimes he even said bad things about the English. He showed scars on his body and insisted on explaining where he had got them. He would end up crying and falling asleep.

Whenever he got a bit of money, M'Baraï would waste it on drink. When he was buying alcohol from the illegal dealers, he'd put all his money on the table when it came time to pay. The trader would help himself generously. M'Baraï would put whatever was left into his pocket.

The friends mutually agreed that Jean M'Baraï was a difficult customer. True, they appreciated his skills as a sailor and fisherman. They would let him stay out of humanity – he didn't have land or a boat and he didn't want to live with the Kanaks – and because they had known him since they were children. But he offended them with his intemperance and the bad stories that he told when he was drunk.

The Chinaman, who was very tolerant when it came to morals and very canny like most of the subjects of the Celestial Empire, wanted, for various reasons, to get close to M'Baraï and make his peace with him. He had strengths he could put to good use. M'Baraï's conciliatory friends mediated to facilitate this connection.

In Jean M'Baraï's eyes, the *China-man* was an important man, "one big fellow master". Just think, he knew how to speak to the Administration and get the gendarmes to come! In doing this, the Celestial man had acquired great prestige and gained a lot of influence over M'Baraï - and even over some of the naïve settlers of the region.

Advised and pushed into it by his friends, M'Baraï accepted the advances of the astute Chinaman. The "Very-Crafty-China-man" sold him a three-ton boat on credit for twice what it was worth. The debt was payable in bêche-de-mer. The buyer of the boat was also obligated to get his provisions from the boat seller. A few vague papers were hastily drawn up in duplicate and signed by the interested parties. In the presence of witnesses, the Chinaman scratched out some characters while the half-caste drew a big, shaky cross. Until the boat had been paid off in full, it was agreed that the port licence would remain in the Chinaman's name.

As a start – so that the debit column really stood out – Jean M'Baraï's account was debited with the cost of the boat, the expenses incurred by the Chinaman in his role as a forced host and the court and bailiff costs that he paid out to get M'Baraï expelled from his property. The supplies and miscellaneous items M'Baraï required for his first expedition were added to this. With this handicap, the half-caste went off to fish for bêche-de-mer, or trepang, or sea cucumber – the name didn't matter - M'Baraï called them "diélos".

Jean M'Baraï fished for "diélos" for pleasure – and he caught a great deal of them. He cut wood – poles and posts – to fulfil profitable contracts made by the Chinaman.

He plied along the coast, transporting goods and picking up the Celestial man's copra. He worked, without killing himself it's true, for months and years, his creditor taking all profits. His account, which he did not understand at all, only grew. However hard he worked, the boat would never be his.

But for all that M'Baraï wasn't unhappy, as he did not plan very far ahead. He was content with making the most of the present. Moreover, he had all he needed to satisfy his, somewhat limited, desires. Look – he had a boat, a popinée, an accordion, a pipe, a spear, a bag of rice and some tea. What more could a man want?

When the weather wasn't good for fishing, he'd spend deliciously lazy days on the sandy islands. Or else he'd go into a quiet bay and live the life of a Sybarite. When he wasn't busy, M'Baraï had the gift of being able to lie on his mat for days and nights, near a fire and in the company of his popinée. He only moved when he grew weary of lying down, or he wanted to eat.

IV

I met M'Baraï not long after his return home. My lifestyle and ways of working pleased him and he considered me to be one of his own. He ended up trusting me implicitly. We finished our fishing campaign before the end of the season and separated as good friends, promising each other we'd meet up again on the islands.

Later, when he was passing in his boat, he'd stop and come to see me in my straw and coconut palm leaf abode – which made him feel at home – and he'd treat me to one of those good old bushman visits, which entailed staying under the host's roof for a few days or for as long as one pleased. Those were the good old days when the struggle for existence was not so tough.

I could recognize his boat from a distance by its sails. When I saw it manœuvering to come and cast anchor in the bay where I lived, I felt happy. As, in these abandoned lands where we live in contemplative solitude without ever seeing a soul, we appreciate the company of the occasional traveller, even if they are poor wretches.

M'Baraï would come ashore with his popinée. He'd walk in front, broad shouldered, stocky yet nimble for all that. He wore sturdy overalls with stitching reinforced by copper rivets. His flared pants covered his bare feet, leaving only his toes visible. He'd come towards me with a smile on his face, his unlit pipe in his mouth, an accordion under his arm and his knife sheathed at his waist.

His popinée, wearing a loose dress dotted with brightly coloured flowers, followed three steps behind him, rolling her hips as she walked. She always carried a basket of woven pandanus leaves over her shoulder. It was a real horn of plenty, both by the volume and diversity of its contents. Look what she had in it: a little square mirror, sticks of tobacco, pieces of cloth, a knife, a Jew's harp, a horn comb, matches, beads, scissors, lengths of string, a harmonica, some small "ouacici" shells, soap, multicoloured wool, Kanak combs, flying fox fur, a razor, knitting needles, pictures cut from newspapers and catalogues, a bottle of cheap scent, and a few coins jumbled in. And I forget what else she had in there. That was the indispensable reticule of Madame M'Baraï.

When the half-caste was only a few steps away from me, his smile would widen, his white teeth standing out against his brown face. His first question for me was invariably whether I was still alive, "You no dead now?" I'd affirm that I was not dead.

He'd laugh silently while holding out his large hand to me. We'd exchange a few simple words and then he'd only speak to answer my questions. His first preoccupation was to find a place to cut his tobacco without scratching the table. And then he'd smoke. When he was outside, he'd shred his tobacco with his fingers.

His popinée stayed in the background – she'd go warm herself in the kitchen or she'd go entertain herself on the beach. She'd either light a little fire or go fishing for us.

I would give M'Baraï a drink and we'd chat a while. Then I'd give him books and illustrated newspapers and I was able to attend to my business.

He would look very carefully at the pictures for a long time, like a well brought up child. Boats, in particular, caught his attention. When he had had enough, he would play his accordion. Regardless of the tune, he always concentrated on the cadence of the bass and would invariably fall into the rhythm of some pilou or another.

Then he'd go for a walk around the out buildings, looking closely at all of the things that were within his realm of understanding and manual capacities. He looked at how this shed, this bread oven, this wheelbarrow, this little boat or this bench had been built. He was especially interested in tools and he'd pick them up to see how they felt in his hands.

Even though he was in an environment where no one gave a toss about manners, M'Baraï would always endeavour to eat properly – European style – which made him awkward and gauche. The poor devil didn't quite know how to use his serviette and he didn't know what some of the utensils on the table were used for. When he was in my company, he kept a check on himself and always asked for water to be put into his wine as he didn't dare serve himself.

In the evening, upon his request, I'd explain the pictures that intrigued him. Afterwards, I'd ask him questions and I'd manage to get him to divulge a few of his past adventures. He'd tell me out of obligation, not pleasure, always coming back to the present which he preferred. He'd tell me about the huge shark he'd speared the day before or about the beautiful gaiacs he'd seen in a valley near the sea, the gusty winds of the North-West Cape, the sardine season at Yandé, the gull egg season on the islets, or the sea cows at Bouarabatch. Then we'd say goodnight and he'd go back to his popinée who was waiting for him in the hut I kept for my friends.

M'Baraï would stay two or three days without taking up much room. Then, without warning, at any time of the day, he'd shake my hand and say, "Me go now. Good bye". And off he'd go with his popinée following in his footsteps.

V

Due to his racial duality and the type of life he had led in his youth, the mind of Jean M'Baraï the half-caste was always hanging in the balance - he was never able to remain stable. He thought and acted at once like a European and a Kanak without being able to distinguish between the two. After all his trials and tribulations – his journeys as a slave trading sailor, his injuries, his sequestration as a breeder in Malekula… after his professional training as a boxer, his life as a black worker in Queensland, not to mention his expulsion from his father's land, his floating mentality was completely cast adrift and he did not know how to guide it towards a lifestyle more in keeping with his European side.

He didn't want to live in a tribe – probably because he had never belonged to one. His mother had left the Poya bush some thirty or more years before, he was unknown to the tribe and he couldn't speak the language. Yet, despite his French blood, he leaned more towards the Kanak way of life, whether due to ease of understanding or a tendency to take the easy way out. His status as a half-caste without a birth certificate, tribe or property, made Jean M'Baraï something of an outcast. He was neither with the whites nor the blacks. He was a sort of Gypsy of the New Caledonian coast.

But for all that, he only worried about it when he had drunk too much alcohol. It was then that he vaguely sensed his status as a pariah among the whites, without really being able to define it. He understood one thing only – they had taken his land and his coconut palms because he wasn't his father's son. However, he was not a Kanak – no, the Administration was wrong there – they were a bunch of liars.

After fishing or having done one of his diverse coastal activities, when he was back at the *China-man's* place, and when the accounts had supposedly been settled, he had the talent of being able to drink as much as he was supposedly in credit. In his drunken state, finding himself back on the property his father had established, he thought about it all again and was moved. The story of his adventures only added to this state of mind – the gunshot wound he'd received, the children he'd fathered in Malekula who were destined to be eaten, the beating the boxers had dished out to him and his work as a *nigger*. And then he'd cry and talk of suicide as he had been hurt by both blacks and whites. He was not aggressive during these alcohol-fuelled bouts of depression. He accused no one, not even the *China-*

man, of his sad state of affairs. But it wouldn't have been wise to rough him up.

One drunken day, when he was particularly inebriated and saddened by his lot, a sobbing M'Baraï shook hands with everyone present and said, "Good bye. Me want finish. Good bye. Me go dead." And he went into a boatshed, took an old rope and tied one end around his neck. Then, holding onto a post, he climbed on a sailmaker's bench and he tied the other end of the rope to a beam and, without a moment's hesitation, jumped off. He was hanging there with a grimace on his face.

But all of those who were there that day followed him. The *Chinaman* was at the front, checking their pace. They then watched him from a distance. After leaving him to swing for a moment with nothing between him and the ground, the Chinaman gave the signal to rescue him. They lifted M'Baraï, untied the rope and put him gently on the ground. Whimpering and crying even louder, M'Baraï scolded his rescuers for not having left him to die. Inconsolable, he rolled in the sandy grass and fell asleep. He got off with a necklace of abrasions.

From this day on, this habit became engrained in M'Baraï. Each time he was really drunk, after the usual *good byes*, he would go and hang himself, always in the same place, and the operation would always follow the same process. His friends would untie him and put him down gently, he'd lie in the grass and cry himself to sleep. It was very funny for the spectators but they soon tired of it and, as the rope never broke, they ended up not finding it amusing anymore.

M'Baraï was the only one not to get sick of it. He must have taken some sort of pleasure in stretching himself like that. One night, he proceeded as usual and went and hanged himself in his usual place. Only one Kanak bothered to follow him. When the operation was done, as soon as the hanged man was swinging and sticking out his tongue, the Kanak cut the rope with his knife. M'Baraï fell heavily on his knees and bit his tongue before falling forward onto his tummy and slamming his face into the ground. Furious, he got up and hit the surprised Kanak with a volley of punches, shouting out in his language, "You pig! You bastard! You hurt me. That's not how I'm usually taken down. You should've lifted me up and put me down gently." That was the last time that M'Baraï hanged himself.

VI

Some time later, some of his acquaintances advised him to leave the Chinaman who was exploiting him like a Kanak. They encouraged him to abandon the boat that he would never own and go to Pam with them where they had negotiated a lucrative long-term contract to supply coral for the limestone used in blast furnaces to make copper. This work suited M'Baraï's abilities and tastes – going onto the reefs at low tide, breaking the coral with a crowbar and dynamite, loading it into a barge at high tide and taking it to its destination. It was still nautical work – he could still spear fish. He followed these men without saying anything to *China-man*.

I never saw M'Baraï again but I asked after him and would get the occasional news.

The coral contract that he was a partner in finished when the factory closed down. Throughout its duration, M'Baraï was unable to control himself. He wasted his money drinking in taverns and getting robbed by the landlords of these dubious nightspots that sprouted like toadstools around the mines and disappeared as soon as the mines did.

Then the half-caste built himself a hut on the edge of the Diahot river. He did so with the consent of the so-called tenant of this government land. The tenant rented him a boat to transport the goods of the few farmers in the area, and his own – for free of course.

As it was everywhere in the bush, amongst the losers and the philosophers of the first period of colonisation, M'Baraï's hut became the refuge and phalanstery of those idle and freewheeling friends who had come to shore in search of an easy life. They were New Caledonian Lazaronis. The community only worked on the days that the steamboat arrived in Pam – twice a month. Then, on sunny days, if they felt like it, they'd go fishing for entertainment.

The popinées, who made the residence more attractive, had more foresight and planted kumara and taro. They gathered honey from the trees and caught crabs and prawns. Little "pocas"[69] followed them like loyal dogs. Pumpkins and edible greens known as "brèdes"

---

69   Pigs, from the English "porker".

grew,[70] sprawling out freely among the lush vegetation. A few little Kanak swamp hens, that were very wary, roamed in the bush around the hut.

The men engaged in more noble occupations. In order to provide meat, they hunted wild pigs and the occasional cow - but on the sly so as not to get into trouble. All of these resources with a bit of rice and tea provided them with sustenance. And some happy days were spent at M'Baraï's cottage.

When the community found itself with a bit of cash (that they'd come by without much effort) they would buy themselves a little treat. This would involve procuring a few litres of wine and rum. Then it was party time – they drank, played the accordion and got rolling drunk for the simple pleasure of getting drunk and engaging in wild antics. The popinées joined in the revelry. They drank too, like men, all the while preaching morals in Kanak and bichelamar. When the drinking spree was at its height, they argued, settled their relationship problems and made jealousy-triggered scenes. Never did they manage to come to an agreement. So it was then very simple – they beat each other up. The weakest, the least aggressive and the popinées, crying like babies and laughing at the same time, took off into the bush. Jean M'Baraï always ruled the roost. It was a Herculean triumph.

The next day all would be forgotten and no one would be bitter. They discussed the blows of the night before and they would laugh about them together.

Sometimes when he was drunk and sad, M'Baraï would be seized by suicidal thoughts again. Before leaving for the other world, he would cry, as would be expected, and say goodbye to all of his friends. Next, he would plunge into the river and disappear under the water. But his swimmer's reflexes and the survival instinct would kick in and bring him back to the surface. Up he'd pop like a cork. Then he'd continue swimming to the bank on the other side and lie on the grass and fall asleep. The next day, he'd swim back across the river and go sheepishly back to his hut.

Hi friends had grown used to seeing him give himself over to these swimming exercises (that were very useful for sobering up) and let him carry on as he pleased, not worrying unduly about him.

One black night, after having bid his friends *adieu*, after having tearfully pressed his popinée to his bosom, Jean M'Baraï plunged into the Diahot River...

That was twenty years ago now. He still has not come back up. He must have dived into eternity.

His popinée claimed to have heard him speak in the rushes at the swamp. It was true, as the purple swamp hens had flown off squawking. And at night she saw him slipping like a shadow through the lantanas and the niaoulis, with their white bark, on the edge of the Diahot.[71] He stopped, stood up like a tree trunk to look at her and signal to her. But she was too afraid and ran away. M'Baraï wanted to pull her to the bottom of the river. When

---

70   "Brède" is a term from the Indian Ocean, which entered into New Caledonia via Reunion Creole-speaking immigrants in the 19th century (for details on this migration see Speedy 2007a, 2007b, 2008, 2009, 2012).
71   Niaouli (Melaleuca quinquenervia) tree found in forests over much of New Caledonia.

it was pitch black, she heard his bare feet walking outside the hut.

In the end, as she couldn't go swimming in the Diahot anymore because she did not want M'Baraï, who had become a devil, to take her, she left the hut and went back to live in her tribe.

And now when the wind blowing down from the mountains sobs in the leaves, when fog slowly creeps along the bottom of the valleys, along the Diahot, and we hear a bird calling "Couwee…" at night, take care! It is not a bird, it is M'Baraï calling his popinée.

BIBLIOGRAPHY

Anderson, Jean. 2006a. *Les Yeux volés* (*Baby No Eyes*, Patricia Grace) with France Grenaudier-Klijn. Papeete: Au Vent des îles.

Anderson, Jean. 2006b. *Electrique cité* (*Electric City*, Patricia Grace) with Anne Magnan-Park. Papeete: Au Vent des îles.

Anderson, Jean. 2007. "Three New Caledonian Poets: translation of work by Nicolas Kurtovitch, Frédéric Ohlen, Paul Wamo" Poetry New Zealand, 35, 10-32.

Anderson, Jean. 2009. *Les Enfants de Ngarua* (*Dogside Story*, Patricia Grace) with France Grenaudier-Klijn. Papeete: Au Vent des îles.

Anderson, Jean. 2010a. "La traduction résistante. Some Principles of Resistant Translation of Francophone and Anglophone Pacific Literature", in Ramsay, Raylene (ed.) Cultural Crossings. Negotiating Identities in Francophone and Anglophone Pacific Literatures / A la croisée des cultures. De la négociation des identités dans les littératures francophones et anglophones du Pacifique. Brussels: Peter Lang, 285-301.

Anderson, Jean. 2010b. *Le Bataillon maori* (*Tu*, Patricia Grace) with France Grenaudier-Klijn. Papeete: Au Vent des îles.

Anderson, Jean. 2012. The Missing King (Le roi absent, Moetai Brotherson). Auckland: Little Island Press.

Armbruster, Stefan. 2013, "South Sea Islanders mark sugar 'slave' days", SBS News, 26 August. http://www.sbs.com.au/news/article/2013/08/16/south-sea-islanders-mark-sugar-slave-days

Arvidson, Ken. 1999/2009. "Passages and Reefs." SPAN Journal of the South Pacific Association for Language and Literary Studies 62, 104-123.

Ashcroft, Bill, Griffiths, Gareth and Tiffin, Helen. 1989. The Empire Writes Back: Theory and Practice in Post-Colonial Literatures. London and New York: Routledge.

Baker, Philip. 1993. "Australian influence on Melanesian Pidgin English", Te Reo, 36, 3-67.

Baker, Philip and Mühlhäusler, Peter. 1996. "The origins and diffusion of Pidgin English in the Pacific", in Wurm, Stephen, Mühlhäusler, Peter and Tryon, Darrell (eds.) Atlas of Languages of Intercultural Communication in the Pacific, Asia and the Americas Vol 2.1. Berlin: Mouton de Gruyter, 551-594.

Bakhtin, Mikhail. 1984. Problems of Dostoevsky's Poetics (translated and edited by Caryl Emmerson). Minneapolis: University of Minnesota Press.

Banaré, Eddy. 2009. "Georges Baudoux", Île en île, Lehman CUNY, published online 28/08/2009, accessed 20/09/2012.
http://www.lehman.cuny.edu/ile.en.ile/paroles/baudoux.html

Banaré, Eddy. 2010. La littérature de la mine en Nouvelle-Calédonie (1853-1953). PhD thesis: Université de la Nouvelle-Calédonie.

Banaré, Eddy. 2012. Les récits du nickel en Nouvelle-Calédonie (1853-1960). Paris, Genève: Honoré Champion.

Banivanua-Mar, Tracey. 2007. Violence and Colonial Dialogue: The Australian-Pacific Indentured Labor Trade. Honolulu: University of Hawai'i Press.

Baudoux, Georges. 1925. Légendes noires. Mœurs canaques. Noumea: A.-L. Laubreaux.

Baudoux, Georges. 1928. Légendes canaques. Paris: Rieder.

Baudoux, Georges. 1952. Légendes canaques 1. Paris: Nouvelles éditions latines.

Baudoux, Georges. 1952. Légendes canaques 2. Paris: Nouvelles éditions latines.

Baudoux, Georges. 1972. Les blancs sont venus. Nouméa: Société d'études historiques de la Nouvelle-Calédonie.

Baudoux, Georges. 1979a. Les blancs sont venus tome 2. Nouméa: Société d'Études Historiques de la Nouvelle-Calédonie.

Baudoux, Georges. 1979b. Il fut un temps…Souvenirs du bagne. Nouméa: Société d'Études Historiques de la Nouvelle-Calédonie.

Baudoux, Georges. 2001. Comment on s'évadait de la Nouvelle-Calédonie. Noumea: Grain de Sable.

Baudoux, Georges. 2009. Les blancs sont venus. Nouméa: Publications de la Société d'Études Historiques de la Nouvelle-Calédonie.

Baudrillard, Jean. 2003. "The Global and the Universal" (translated by Deborah Walker and Raylene Ramsay), in Grace, Victoria, Worth, Heather and Simmons, Laurence (eds.), Baudrillard West of the Dateline. Palmerston North: Dunmore Press, 23-36.

Bensa, Alban and Leblic, Isabelle (eds.). 2000. En pays kanak: ethnologie, linguistique, archéologie, histoire de la Nouvelle-Calédonie. Paris: Éditions de la Maison des sciences de l'homme.

Bensa, Alban. 2006. La fin de l'exotisme. Essais d'anthropologie critiques. Toulouse: Anacharsis.

Bensa, Alban, Goromoedo, Yvan and Muckle, Adrian. 2015. Les sanglots de l'aigle pêcheur. Nouvelle-Calédonie: la guerre kanak de 1917. Toulouse: Anacharsis.

Brou, Bernard. 1980. "Un cas de vérité historique chez Baudoux", Bulletin de la Société d'Études Historiques de la Nouvelle-Calédonie, 43, 47-56.

Derrida, Jacques. 1998. Monolingualism of the Other: Or, The Prosthesis of Origin. Translated by Patrick Mensah. Stanford: Stanford University Press.

Docker, Edward Wybergh. 1981. The Blackbirders: A brutal story of the Kanaka slave-trade. Sydney: Angus & Robertson.

Gasser, Bernard. 1992. "Le contact entre Européens et Canaques dans les nouvelles de Georges Baudoux", in Pérez, Michel (ed.), Voyage, découverte, colonisation, Actes du cinquième Colloque CORAIL. Noumea: CORAIL, 145-164.

Gasser, Bernard. 1996. Georges Baudoux: la quête de la vérité. Noumea: Grain de Sable.

Gorodé, Déwé, Kurtovitch, Nicolas, Ramsay, Raylene, and McKay, Brian. 1999. Dire le vrai / To Tell the Truth translated and postface by Raylene Ramsay and Brian Mackay. Nouméa: Grain de Sable.

Gorodé, Déwé, and Brown, Peter. 2004. The Kanak apple season: selected short fiction of Dewe Gorodé / translated and edited by Peter Brown. Canberra: Pandanus Books.

Gorodé, Déwé, Ramsay, Raylene, Walker, Deborah, and Brown, Peter. 2004. Sharing as custom provides: selected poems of Dewe Gorode / translated and edited by Raylene Ramsay and Deborah Walker. Canberra: Pandanus Books.

Gorodé, Déwé, and Ramsay, Raylene, and Walker, Deborah. 2011. The Wreck / translated and with a critical introduction by Raylene Ramsay and Deborah Walker. Auckland: Little Island Press.

Hau'ofa, Epeli. 1994. "Our Sea of Islands", The Contemporary Pacific, 6.1, 147–161.

Hollyman, Keith J. 1959. "Polynesian influence in New Caledonia", The Journal of the Polynesian Society, 68.4, 357-389.

Hollyman, Keith J. 2000a. "Les pidgins anglais et français de la région calédonienne", Observatoire du Français dans le Pacifique – Études et documents, 13, 25-64.

Hollyman, Keith J. 2000b. "Français calédonien: le pidgin français, le 'français canaque' de Baudoux, le tayo de Saint-Louis, le français du Midi et le français colonial d'Algérie", Observatoire du Français dans le Pacifique – Études et documents, 13, 89-104.

Hunt, Doug. 2007. "Hunting the Blackbirder: Ross Lewin and the Royal Navy", Journal of Pacific History, 42.1, 37-53.

Hunt, Doug and Kennedy, K.H. 2006. "Bye bye blackbirder: the death of Ross Lewin", Journal of the Royal Historical Society of Queensland, 19.5, (2006), 805-823.

Ingram, Charmaine. 2013. "South Sea Islanders call for an apology", ABC Lateline News, 2 September. http://www.abc.net.au/lateline/content/2013/s3839465.htm

Laubreaux, Alin. 1928. Yann-le-métis. Paris: Albin Michel.

Leenhardt, Maurice. 1986. Gens de la Grande Terre. Paris: Ed. du Cagou.

Lévy-Bruhl, Lucien. 1922. La mentalité primitive. Paris: Félix Alcan.

Mariotti, Jean. 1939. Contes de Poindi. New York: Domino Press.

Mariotti, Jean and Averill, Esther Holden. 1938. Tales of Poindi / translated by Esther Holden Averill. New York: Domino Press.

Martin, Alain. 1995a. La représentation du monde canaque dans l'œuvre de Georges Baudoux (1870-1949), PhD thesis: l'Université de Paris VIII.

Martin, Alain. 1995b. "La 'mise en scène' de la parole canaque dans les Légendes canaques de Georges Baudoux (1870-1949)", in Angleviel, Frédéric (ed.) Parole, communication et symbole en Océanie, Actes du septième Colloque CORAIL. Paris: L'Harmattan, 71-91.

Meakins, Felicity. 2014. "Language contact varieties", in Koch, Harold and Nordlinger, Rachel (eds.) The languages and linguistics of Australia: a comprehensive guide. Berlin: Mouton de Gruyter, 365-416.

Moore, Clive. 1992. "Revising the revisionists: the historiography of immigrant Melanesians in Australia", Pacific Studies, 15.2, 61–86.

Mortensen, Reid. 2000. "Slaving in Australian Courts: Blackbirding Cases, 1869-1871", Journal of South Pacific Law 4.
http://www.paclii.org/journals/fJSPL/vol04/7.shtml

Munro, Doug. 1995. "The Labor Trade in Melanesians to Queensland: An Historiographic Essay", *Journal of Social History*, 28.3, 609-627.

O'Reilly, Patrick. 1949. "Les différentes éditions des Contes de Poindi de Jean Mariotti", Journal de la Société des océanistes, 5, 191-192.

O'Reilly, Patrick. 1950. "Georges Baudoux prospecteur et écrivain calédonien", Journal de la société des océanistes, 6, 185-206.

Ramsay, Raylene. 2014. The Literatures of the French Pacific: Reconfiguring Hybridity. Liverpool: Liverpool University Press.

Ramsay, Raylene and Walker, Deborah. 2010. "Translating Hybridity: The Curious Case of the first Kanak novel (Déwé Gorodé's L'épave)", The AALITRA Review: A Journal of Literary Translation, 1, 44-57.
http://www.nla.gov.au/openpublish/index.php/ALLITRA/article/viewFile/1736/2116

Ramsay, Raylene and Walker, Deborah (eds.). 2011. Nights of Storytelling. A Cultural History of Kanaky / New Caledonia. Honolulu: University of Hawai'i Press.

Savoie, Hélène and Ramsland, Marie. 1998. Voiles blanches sables rouges / White Wings Red Sands / translated by Marie Ramsland. Noumea: Éditions du Lagon.

Scarr, Deryck 1967. "Recruits and Recruiters: A Portrait of the Pacific Islands Labour Trade", The Journal of Pacific History, 2.1, 5–24.

Shineberg, Dorothy. 1967. They came for sandalwood: a study of the sandalwood trade in the south-west Pacific, 1830-1865. London, New York: Melbourne University Press, Cambridge University Press.

Shineberg, Dorothy. 1999. The people trade: Pacific Island laborers and New Caledonia, 1865-1930. Honolulu: University of Hawai'i Press.

Smith, Norval. 2015. "Substrate phonology, superstrate phonology and adstrate phonology in creole languages", in Muysken, Pieter and Smith, Norval (eds.) Surviving the Middle Passage: The West Africa-Suriname Sprachbund. Berlin: de Gruyter.

Solier, Alain. 1996. "Preface" in Gasser, Bernard. Georges Baudoux: la quête de la vérité. Noumea: Grain de Sable, 4-5.

Speedy, Karin. 2003. "Translating Socrates' 'Creole' in Georges Baudoux's Sauvages et Civilisés", Metamorphoses. Special Issue on Francophone Literature, 11.1, 120-132.

Speedy, Karin. 2005. "Les parlers du Créole et du Tonkinois dans Sauvages et Civilisés de Baudoux : authentiques ou stéréotypés ?", in Fillol, Véronique and Vernaudon, Jacques (eds.) Stéréotypes et représentations en Océanie, Actes du 17ème Colloque CORAIL. Nouméa: Corail/Editions Grain de Sable, 107-124.

Speedy, Karin. 2006. "'Naturam expelles furca tamen usque recurret': Exploring the Ambiguity behind the Notions of "Savage" and "Civilised" in Baudoux's Colonial New Caledonia", Essays in French Literature, 43, 217-235.

Speedy, Karin. 2007a. "Reunion Creole in New Caledonia: What influence on Tayo?" Journal of Pidgin and Creole Languages 22.2, 193-230.

Speedy, Karin. 2007b. Colons, Créoles et Coolies: L'immigration réunionnaise en Nouvelle-Calédonie (XIXe siècle) et le tayo de Saint-Louis. Paris: L'Harmattan.

Speedy, Karin. 2008. "Out of the frying pan and into the fire: Reunionese immigrants and the sugar industry in nineteenth-century New Caledonia", New Zealand Journal of French Studies 29.2, 5-19.

Speedy, Karin. 2009. "Who were the Reunion Coolies of Nineteenth-Century New Caledonia?", Journal of Pacific History 44.2, 123-140.

Speedy, Karin. 2010. "Memories, Myths and Métissage as Means of Negotiating Identity in Hélène Savoie's Les terres de la demi-lune", in Ramsay, Raylene (ed.) Cultural Crossings. Negotiating Identities in Francophone and Anglophone Pacific Literatures / A la croisée des cultures. De la négociation des identités dans les littératures francophones et anglophones du Pacifique. Brussels: Peter Lang, 181-195.

Speedy, Karin and Savoie, Hélène. 2010. Les terres de la demi-lune / Half-moon lands / translated and with a critical introduction by Karin Speedy. Paris: L'Harmattan.

Speedy, Karin. 2012. "From the Indian Ocean to the Pacific: Affranchis and Petits-Blancs in New Caledonia", Portal Journal of Multidisciplinary International Studies, Special Issue: Indian Ocean Traffic.
http://epress.lib.uts.edu.au/journals/index.php/portal/article/view/2567

Speedy, Karin. 2013a. "'After me fellow caïcaï you': Eating the Other / The Other eating", Portal Journal of Multidisciplinary International Studies, Special Issue: Edible Alterity.
http://epress.lib.uts.edu.au/journals/index.php/portal/article/view/2971

Speedy, Karin. 2013b. "Reflections on creole genesis in New Caledonia", Acta Linguistica Hafniensia, 45.2, 187-205.

Speedy, Karin. 2015a. "The Sutton Case: The First Franco-Australian Foray into Blackbirding", Journal of Pacific History, 50.3, 344-364.
http://dx.doi.org/10.1080/00223344.2015.1073868

Speedy, Karin. 2015b. "Pacific Literature in Translation: Bringing Francophone and Anglophone Voices Together" in Francesco Benocci and Marco Sonzogni (eds.), Translation, Transnationalism and World Literature. Essays in Translation Studies (2011-2014). Novi Ligure: Edizioni Joker, 313-330.

Spitz, Chantal and Anderson, Jean. 2007. Island of Shattered Dreams / Chantal Spitz, L'île des reves écrasés, translated by Jean Anderson. Wellington: Huia.

Stewart, Frank, Mateatea-Allain, Kareva and Dale, Alexander (eds.). 2006. Varua Tupu: New Writing from French Polynesia. Honolulu: University of Hawai'i Press.

Sugar Slaves. 1995. A film made by Film Australia and the ABC, executive producer Sharon Connolly, director/co-producer Trevor Graham, producer, Penny Robins. Available on DVD.

Te Punga Somerville, Alice. 2012. Once Were Pacific: Māori Connections to Oceania. Minneapolis: University of Minnesota Press.

Troy, Jakelin. 1994. Melaleuka: a history and description of New South Wales Pidgin. PhD thesis: Australian National University.

Venuti, Lawrence. 1998. The Scandals of Translation. London, New York: Routledge.

RECOMMENDED READING IN ENGLISH

BLACKBIRDING AND THE PACIFIC LABOUR TRADE

Banivanua-Mar, Tracey. 2007. Violence and Colonial Dialogue: The Australian-Pacific Indentured Labor Trade. Honolulu: University of Hawai'i Press.

Bird, Wal. 2005. Me No Go Mally Bulla: Recruiting & Blackbirding in the Queensland Labour Trade 1863-1906. Charnwood: Ginninderra Press.

Corris, Peter. 1970. "Pacific Island labour migrants in Queensland", The Journal of Pacific History, 5.1, 43-64.

Corris, Peter. 1973. Passage, Port and Plantation: A History of the Solomon Islands Labour Migration, 1870–1914. Melbourne: Melbourne University Press.

Diamond, Marion. 1988. The Sea Horse and the Wanderer: Ben Boyd in Australia. Melbourne: Melbourne University Press.

Docker, Edward Wybergh. 1981. The Blackbirders: A brutal story of the Kanaka slave-trade. Sydney: Angus & Robertson

Evans, Raymond, Saunders, Kay and Kathryn Cronin. 1993. Race Relations in Colonial Queensland: A history of exclusion, exploitation and extermination. St. Lucia: University of Queensland Press.

Hunt, Doug. 2007. "Hunting the Blackbirder: Ross Lewin and the Royal Navy", Journal of Pacific History, 42.1, 37-53.

Lal, Brij V., Munro, Doug and Beechert, Edward D. (eds.). 1993. Plantation Workers: Resistance and Accommodation. Honolulu: University of Hawaii Press.

Maude, Henry Evans. 1981. Slavers in Paradise. The Peruvian Slave Trade in Polynesia, 1862-1864. Canberra: Australian National University Press.

Moore, Clive, Leckie, Jacqueline and Munro, Doug (eds.). 1990. Labour in the South Pacific. Townsville: James Cook University of Northern Queensland.

Mortensen, Reid. 2000. "Slaving in Australian Courts: Blackbirding Cases, 1869-1871", Journal of South Pacific Law 4.
http://www.paclii.org/journals/fJSPL/vol04/7.shtml

Munro, Doug. 1993. "The Pacific Islands Labour Trade: Approaches, Methodologies, Debates", Slavery and Abolition, 14.2, 87-108.

Munro, Doug. 1995. "The Labor Trade in Melanesians to Queensland: An Historiographic Essay", Journal of Social History, 28.3, 609-627.

Saunders, Kay. 1982. Workers in Bondage: The Origins and Bases of Unfree Labour in Queensland 1824-1916. St. Lucia: University of Queensland Press. http://www.textqueensland.com.au/item/book/c031aa5fd0f8cf8038c4262acf82b7c5

Shineberg, Dorothy. 1967. They came for sandalwood: a study of the sandalwood trade in the south-west Pacific, 1830-1865. London, New York: Melbourne University Press, Cambridge University Press.

Shineberg, Dorothy. 1991. "'Noumea No Good. Noumea No Pay': 'New Hebridean' Indentured Labour in New Caledonia, 1865-1925", Journal of Pacific History, 26.2, 187-205.

Shineberg, Dorothy. 1999. The people trade: Pacific Island laborers and New Caledonia, 1865-1930. Honolulu: University of Hawai'i Press.

Speedy, Karin. 2015. "The Sutton Case: The First Franco-Australian Foray into Blackbirding", Journal of Pacific History, 50.3, 344-364. http://dx.doi.org/10.1080/00223344.2015.1073868

Thomas, Nicholas. 2010. Islanders: the Pacific in the age of empire. New Haven: Yale University Press.

FRANCOPHONE PACIFIC LITERATURE IN TRANSLATION

Anderson, Jean. 2007. "Three New Caledonian Poets: translation of work by Nicolas Kurtovitch, Frédéric Ohlen, Paul Wamo" Poetry New Zealand, 35, 10-32.

Anderson, Jean. 2012. The Missing King (Le roi absent, Moetai Brotherson). Auckland: Little Island Press.

Gorodé, Déwé, Kurtovitch, Nicolas, Ramsay, Raylene, and McKay, Brian. 1999. Dire le vrai / To Tell the Truth translated and postface by Raylene Ramsay and Brian Mackay. Nouméa: Grain de Sable.

Gorodé, Déwé, and Brown, Peter. 2004. The Kanak apple season: selected short fiction of Dewe Gorodé / translated and edited by Peter Brown. Canberra: Pandanus Books.

Gorodé, Déwé, Ramsay, Raylene, Walker, Deborah, and Brown, Peter. 2004. Sharing as custom provides: selected poems of Dewe Gorode / translated and edited by Raylene Ramsay and Deborah Walker. Canberra: Pandanus Books.

Gorodé, Déwé, and Ramsay, Raylene, and Walker, Deborah. 2011. The Wreck / translated and with a critical introduction by Raylene Ramsay and Deborah Walker. Auckland: Little Island Press.

Ramsay, Raylene. 2014. The Literatures of the French Pacific: Reconfiguring Hybridity. Liverpool: Liverpool University Press.

Ramsay, Raylene and Walker, Deborah (eds.). 2011. Nights of Storytelling. A Cultural History of Kanaky / New Caledonia. Honolulu: University of Hawai'i Press.

Savoie, Hélène and Ramsland, Marie. 1998. Voiles blanches sables rouges / White Wings Red Sands / translated by Marie Ramsland. Noumea: Éditions du Lagon.

Savoie, Hélène and Speedy, Karin. 2010. Les terres de la demi-lune / Half-moon lands / translated and with a critical introduction by Karin Speedy. Paris: L'Harmattan.

Spitz, Chantal T. and Anderson, Jean. 2007. Island of Shattered Dreams / Chantal Spitz, L'île des reves écrasés, translated by Jean Anderson. Wellington: Huia.

Stewart, Frank, Mateatea-Allain, Kareva and Dale, Alexander (eds.). 2006. Varua Tupu: New Writing from French Polynesia. Honolulu: University of Hawai'i Press.

PACIFIC CONTACT LANGUAGES

Baker, Philip. 1993. "Australian influence on Melanesian Pidgin English", Te Reo, 36, 3-67.

Baker, Philip and Mühlhäusler, Peter. 1996. "The origins and diffusion of Pidgin English in the Pacific", in Wurm, Stephen, Mühlhäusler, Peter and Tryon, Darrell (eds.) Atlas of Languages of Intercultural Communication in the Pacific, Asia and the Americas Vol 2.1. Berlin: Mouton de Gruyter, 551-594.

Clark, Ross. 1979. "In Search of Beach-la-Mar: Towards a History of Pacific Pidgin English", Te Reo, 22, 3–64.

Crowley, Terry. 1990. Beach-la-Mar to Bislama: the emergence of a national language in Vanuatu. Oxford, New York: Clarendon Press, Oxford University Press.

Drechsel, Emanuel J. 2014. Language Contact in the Early Colonial Pacific. Cambridge Approaches to Language Contact. Cambridge: Cambridge University Press. http://dx.doi.org/10.1017/CBO9781139057561

Hollyman, Keith J. 1959. "Polynesian influence in New Caledonia", The Journal of the Polynesian Society, 68.4, 357-389.

Keesing, Roger. 1988. Melanesian Pidgin and the Oceanic Substrate. Stanford: Stanford University Press.

Lynch, John. 1998. Pacific Languages: An Introduction. Honolulu: University of Hawai'i Press.

Meakins, Felicity. 2014. "Language contact varieties", in Koch, Harold and Nordlinger, Rachel (eds.) The languages and linguistics of Australia: a comprehensive guide. Berlin: Mouton de Gruyter, 365-416.

Mühlhäusler, Peter. 1991. "Queensland Kanaka English", in Romaine, Suzanne (ed.) Language in Australia. Cambridge: Cambridge University Press, 174-179.

Siegel, Jeff. 2008. The Emergence of Pidgin and Creole Languages. Oxford: Oxford University Press.

Siegel, Jeff. 2010. "Contact Languages of the Pacific", in Hickey, Raymond (ed.) The Handbook of Language Contact. Chichester: Wiley-Blackwell, 814–836.

Speedy, Karin. 2013b. "Reflections on creole genesis in New Caledonia", Acta Linguistica Hafniensia, 45.2, 187-205.

Troy, Jakelin. 1994. Melaleuka: a history and description of New South Wales Pidgin. PhD thesis: Australian National University.

Tryon, Darrell T. and Charpentier, Jean-Michel. 2004. Pacific Pidgins and Creoles. Berlin: de Gruyter.

PACIFIC HISTORY

Aldrich, Robert. 1990. The French Presence in the South Pacific, 1842-1940. Basingstoke, Hampshire: Macmillan.

Aldrich, Robert. 1991. France, Oceania and Australia, Past and Present. Australia: Dept. of Economic History, University of Sydney.

Creed, Barbara and Hoorn, Jeanette. 2001. Body trade: captivity, cannibalism and colonialism in the Pacific. Annandale, New York: Pluto Press, Routledge.

Denoon, Donald, Malama Meleisea, Stewart Firth, Jocelyn Linnekin, and Karen Nero (eds.). 1997. The Cambridge History of the Pacific Islanders. Cambridge, Sydney: Cambridge University Press.

Douglas, Bronwen. 1998. Across the Great Divide: Journeys in History and Anthropology. Amsterdam: Harwood Academic Publishers.

Foucrier, Annick. 2005. The French and the Pacific World, 17th-19th Centuries: Explorations, Migrations, and Cultural Exchanges. Aldershot: Ashgate.

Hau'ofa, Epeli. 1994. "Our Sea of Islands", The Contemporary Pacific, 6.1, 147–161.

Howe, Kerry. 1984. Where the Waves Fall: A New South Seas Island History from First Settlement to Colonial Rule. Honolulu: University of Hawaii Press.

Jolly, Margaret, Tcherkézoff, Serge and Tryon, Darrell. 2009. Oceanic encounters: exchange, desire, violence. Canberra: ANU E Press. http://epress.anu.edu.au/

Lal, Brij V. and Fortune, Kate (eds.). 2000. The Pacific Islands: An Encyclopedia. Honolulu: University of Hawaii Press.

Thomas, Nicholas. 2010. Islanders: the Pacific in the age of empire. New Haven: Yale University Press.

Lyons, Martyn. 1986. The Totem and the Tricolour: a Short History of New Caledonia since 1774. Kensington: New South Wales University Press.

Scarr, Deryck. 1990. The history of the Pacific Islands: kingdoms of the reefs. South Melbourne: Macmillan.

AUTHOR BIOGRAPHY

Dr Karin Speedy is an Associate Professor and Head of French and Francophone Studies at Macquarie University in Sydney, Australia. Karin's research focuses on historical, cultural, linguistic and literary links between peoples and communities of the Pacific and Indian Oceans, and in particular, interrogates the juncture between the colonial and postcolonial francophone and anglophone worlds.

Karin has authored three books (Les Terres de la demi-lune/Half-moon Lands (2010) with Hélène Savoie, Everyone Speaks English, Right? (2008) and Colons, créoles et coolies (2007)) and numerous book chapters, journal articles and conference papers. She is dedicated to introducing and promoting francophone literature to the English-speaking Pacific (and beyond) thus enabling cultural and literary exchange between peoples of the region.

In 2013, Karin received the John Dunmore Medal (New Zealand Federation of Alliances Françaises) in recognition of her outstanding contribution to the knowledge of the history of New Caledonia and French Creole language in the Pacific.

For more information about Karin and her publications see
https://mq.academia.edu/KarinSpeedy

or

https://www.mq.edu.au/about_us/faculties_and_departments/faculty_of_arts/department_of_international_studies/staff/staff_eurolang/associate_professor_karin_speedy/

www.ingramcontent.com/pod-product-compliance
Lightning Source LLC
Chambersburg PA
CBHW041753010726
47507CB00009B/381